WAR AND PEACE
BOOK SEVEN : 1810-11

By Leo Tolstoy

Double 9
BOOKS

War and Peace Book 7
by Leo Tolstoy

ISBN: 978-93-94973-91-6

Published by

DOUBLE 9 BOOKS

2/13-B, Ansari Road
Daryaganj, New Delhi - 110002
info@double9books.com
www.double9books.com
Tel. 011-40042856

Printed in India.

About the Author

Leo Tolstoy was a Russian creator known for his books War and Peace which is viewed as the best book of pragmatist fiction. Tolstoy is additionally viewed as world's best author by quite a few people. Additionally an ethical scholar and a social reformer, Tolstoy had extreme moralistic points of view. In later life, he turned into an intense Christian rebel and anarcho-conservative.

Leo Tolstoy Born in Yasnaya Polyana on September 9, 1828, He had a place with a notable honorable Russian family. He was the fourth among five offspring of Count Nikolai Ilyich Tolstoy and Countess Mariya Tolstaya, both of whom kicked the bucket passing on their youngsters to be raised by family members.

In 1844, Tolstoy was acknowledged into Kazan University. Incapable to graduate past the subsequent year, Tolstoy got back to Yasnava Polyana and afterward invested energy going among Moscow and St. Petersburg. With some functioning information on a few dialects, he turned into a multilingual. Yet again the recently observed youth pulled in Tolstoy towards drinking, visiting massage parlors and most betting which left him in weighty obligation and anguish however Tolstoy before long acknowledged he was carrying on with a brutish life and endeavored college tests with the expectation that he would acquire a situation with the public authority, yet finished yet up in Caucuses serving in the military continuing in the strides of his senior sibling.

In Year 1862, Leo Tolstoy wedded Sophia Andreevna Behrs, generally called Sonya, who was 16 years more youthful than him. The couple had thirteen youngsters, of which, five passed on at an early age. Sonya went about as

Tolstoy's secretary, editor and monetary chief while he made two out of his most prominent works. Their initial wedded life was loaded up with happiness.

He started composing his show-stopper, War and Peace in 1862. The six volumes of the work were distributed somewhere in the range of 1863 and 1869. With 580 characters got from history and others made by Tolstoy, this extraordinary novel takes on investigating the hypothesis of history and the irrelevance of noted figures like Alexander and Napoleon. Anna Karenina, Tolstoy's next epic was begun in 1873 and distributed totally in 1878.

Contents

BOOK SEVEN : 1810-11

CHAPTER I

The Bible legend tells us that the absence of labor—idleness— was a condition of the first man's blessedness before the Fall. Fallen man has retained a love of idleness, but the curse weighs on the race not only because we have to seek our bread in the sweat of our brows, but because our moral nature is such that we cannot be both idle and at ease. An inner voice tells us we are in the wrong if we are idle. If man could find a state in which he felt that though idle he was fulfilling his duty, he would have found one of the conditions of man's primitive blessedness. And such a state of obligatory and irreproachable idleness is the lot of a whole class—the military. The chief attraction of military service has consisted and will consist in this compulsory and irreproachable idleness.

Nicholas Rostóv experienced this blissful condition to the full when, after 1807, he continued to serve in the Pávlograd regiment, in which he already commanded the squadron he had taken over from Denísov.

Rostóv had become a bluff, good-natured fellow, whom his Moscow acquaintances would have considered rather bad form, but who was liked and respected by his comrades, subordinates, and superiors, and was well contented with his life. Of late, in 1809, he found in letters from home more frequent complaints from his mother that their affairs were falling into greater and greater disorder, and that it was time for him to come back to gladden and comfort his old parents.

Reading these letters, Nicholas felt a dread of their wanting to take him away from surroundings in which, protected from all the entanglements of life, he was living so calmly and quietly. He felt that sooner or later he would have to re-enter that whirlpool of life, with its embarrassments and affairs to be straightened out, its accounts with stewards, quarrels, and intrigues, its ties, society, and with Sónya's love and his promise to her. It was all dreadfully difficult and complicated; and he replied to his mother in cold, formal letters in French, beginning: "My dear Mamma," and ending: "Your obedient son," which said nothing of when he would return. In 1810 he received letters from his parents, in which they told him of Natásha's engagement to Bolkónski, and that the wedding would be in a year's time because the old prince made difficulties. This letter grieved and mortified Nicholas. In the first place he was sorry that Natásha, for whom he cared more than for anyone else in the family, should be lost to the home; and secondly, from his hussar point of view, he regretted not to have been there to show that fellow Bolkónski that connection with him was no such great honor after all, and that if he loved Natásha he might dispense with permission from his dotard father. For a moment he hesitated whether he should not apply for leave in order to see Natásha before she was married, but then came the maneuvers, and considerations about Sónya and about the confusion of their affairs, and Nicholas again put it off. But in the spring of that year, he received a letter from his mother, written without his father's knowledge, and that letter persuaded him to return. She wrote that if he did not come and take matters in hand, their whole property would be sold by auction and they would all have to go begging. The count was so weak, and trusted Mítenka so much, and was so good-natured, that everybody took advantage of him and things were going from bad to worse. "For God's sake, I implore you, come at once if you do not wish to make me and the whole family wretched," wrote the countess.

This letter touched Nicholas. He had that common sense of a matter-of-fact man which showed him what he ought to do.

The right thing now was, if not to retire from the service, at any rate to go home on leave. Why he had to go he did not know; but after his after-dinner nap he gave orders to saddle Mars, an extremely vicious gray stallion that had not been ridden for a long time, and when he returned with the horse all in a lather, he informed Lavrúshka (Denísov's servant who had remained with him) and his comrades who turned up in the evening that he was applying for leave and was going home. Difficult and strange as it was for him to reflect that he would go away without having heard from the staff—and this interested him extremely—whether he was promoted to a captaincy or would receive the Order of St. Anne for the last maneuvers; strange as it was to think that he would go away without having sold his three roans to the Polish Count Golukhovski, who was bargaining for the horses Rostóv had betted he would sell for two thousand rubles; incomprehensible as it seemed that the ball the hussars were giving in honor of the Polish Mademoiselle Przazdziecka (out of rivalry to the Uhlans who had given one in honor of their Polish Mademoiselle Borzozowska) would take place without him—he knew he must go away from this good, bright world to somewhere where everything was stupid and confused. A week later he obtained his leave. His hussar comrades—not only those of his own regiment, but the whole brigade—gave Rostóv a dinner to which the subscription was fifteen rubles a head, and at which there were two bands and two choirs of singers. Rostóv danced the Trepák with Major Básov; the tipsy officers tossed, embraced, and dropped Rostóv; the soldiers of the third squadron tossed him too, and shouted "hurrah!" and then they put him in his sleigh and escorted him as far as the first post station.

During the first half of the journey—from Kremenchúg to Kiev—all Rostóv's thoughts, as is usual in such cases, were behind him, with the squadron; but when he had gone more than halfway he began to forget his three roans and Dozhoyvéyko, his quartermaster, and to wonder anxiously how things would be at Otrádnoe and what he would find there. Thoughts of home grew stronger the nearer he approached it—far stronger, as though this feeling of his was subject to the law by which the force of attraction is in inverse proportion to the square of the distance. At the last post station before Otrádnoe he gave the driver a three-ruble tip, and on arriving he ran breathlessly, like a boy, up the steps of his home.

After the rapture of meeting, and after that odd feeling of unsatisfied expectation—the feeling that "everything is just the same, so why did I hurry?"—Nicholas began to settle down in his old home world. His father and mother were much the same, only a little older. What was new in them was a certain uneasiness and occasional discord, which there used not to be, and which, as Nicholas soon found out, was due to the bad state of their affairs. Sónya was nearly twenty; she had stopped growing prettier and promised nothing more than she was already, but that was enough. She exhaled happiness and love from the time Nicholas returned, and the faithful, unalterable love of this girl had a gladdening effect on him. Pétya and Natásha surprised Nicholas most. Pétya was a big handsome boy of thirteen, merry, witty, and mischievous, with a voice that was already breaking. As for Natásha, for a long while Nicholas wondered and laughed whenever he looked at her.

"You're not the same at all," he said.

"How? Am I uglier?"

"On the contrary, but what dignity? A princess!" he whispered to her.

"Yes, yes, yes!" cried Natásha, joyfully.

She told him about her romance with Prince Andrew and of his visit to Otrádnoe and showed him his last letter.

"Well, are you glad?" Natásha asked. "I am so tranquil and happy now."

"Very glad," answered Nicholas. "He is an excellent fellow.... And are you very much in love?"

"How shall I put it?" replied Natásha. "I was in love with Borís, with my teacher, and with Denísov, but this is quite different. I feel at peace and settled. I know that no better man than he exists, and I am calm and contented now. Not at all as before."

Nicholas expressed his disapproval of the postponement of the marriage for a year; but Natásha attacked her brother with exasperation, proving to him that it could not be otherwise, and that it would be a bad thing to enter a family against the father's will, and that she herself wished it so.

"You don't at all understand," she said.

Nicholas was silent and agreed with her.

Her brother often wondered as he looked at her. She did not seem at all like a girl in love and parted from her affianced husband. She was even-tempered and calm and quite as cheerful as of old. This amazed Nicholas and even made him regard Bolkónski's courtship skeptically. He could not believe that her fate was sealed, especially as he had not seen her with Prince Andrew. It always seemed to him that there was something not quite right about this intended marriage.

"Why this delay? Why no betrothal?" he thought. Once, when he had touched on this topic with his mother, he discovered, to his surprise and somewhat to his satisfaction, that in the depth of her soul she too had doubts about this marriage.

"You see he writes," said she, showing her son a letter of Prince Andrew's, with that latent grudge a mother always has in regard to a daughter's future married happiness, "he writes that he won't come before December. What can be keeping him? Illness, probably! His health is very delicate. Don't tell Natásha. And don't attach importance to her being so bright: that's because she's living through the last days of her girlhood, but I know what she is like every time we receive a letter from him! However, God grant that everything turns out well!" (She always ended with these words.) "He is an excellent man!"

CHAPTER II

After reaching home Nicholas was at first serious and even dull. He was worried by the impending necessity of interfering in the stupid business matters for which his mother had called him home. To throw off this burden as quickly as possible, on the third day after his arrival he went, angry and scowling and without answering questions as to where he was going, to Mítenka's lodge and demanded an *account of everything*. But what an *account of everything* might be Nicholas knew even less than the frightened and bewildered Mítenka. The conversation and the examination of the accounts with Mítenka did not last long. The village elder, a peasant delegate, and the village clerk, who were waiting in the passage, heard with fear and delight first the young count's voice roaring and snapping and rising louder and louder, and then words of abuse, dreadful words, ejaculated one after the other.

"Robber!... Ungrateful wretch!... I'll hack the dog to pieces! I'm not my father!... Robbing us!..." and so on.

Then with no less fear and delight they saw how the young count, red in the face and with bloodshot eyes, dragged Mítenka out by the scruff of the neck and applied his foot and knee to his behind with great agility at convenient moments between the words, shouting, "Be off! Never let me see your face here again, you villain!"

Mítenka flew headlong down the six steps and ran away into the shrubbery. (This shrubbery was a well-known haven of refuge for culprits at Otrádnoe. Mítenka himself, returning tipsy from the town, used to hide there, and many of the residents at Otrádnoe, hiding from Mítenka, knew of its protective qualities.)

Mítenka's wife and sisters-in-law thrust their heads and frightened faces out of the door of a room where a bright samovar was boiling and where the steward's high bedstead stood with its patchwork quilt.

The young count paid no heed to them, but, breathing hard, passed by with resolute strides and went into the house.

The countess, who heard at once from the maids what had happened at the lodge, was calmed by the thought that now their affairs would certainly improve, but on the other hand felt anxious as to the effect this excitement might have on her son. She went several times to his door on tiptoe and listened, as he lighted one pipe after another.

Next day the old count called his son aside and, with an embarrassed smile, said to him:

"But you know, my dear boy, it's a pity you got excited! Mítenka has told me all about it."

"I knew," thought Nicholas, "that I should never understand anything in this crazy world."

"You were angry that he had not entered those 700 rubles. But they were carried forward—and you did not look at the other page."

"Papa, he is a blackguard and a thief! I know he is! And what I have done, I have done; but, if you like, I won't speak to him again."

"No, my dear boy" (the count, too, felt embarrassed. He knew he had mismanaged his wife's property and was to blame toward his children, but he did not know how to remedy it). "No, I beg you to attend to the business. I am old. I..."

"No, Papa. Forgive me if I have caused you unpleasantness. I understand it all less than you do."

"Devil take all these peasants, and money matters, and carryings forward from page to page," he thought. "I used to understand what a 'corner' and the stakes at cards meant, but carrying forward to another page I don't understand at all," said he to himself, and after that he did not meddle in business affairs. But once the countess called her son and informed him that she had a promissory note from Anna Mikháylovna for two thousand rubles, and asked him what he thought of doing with it.

"This," answered Nicholas. "You say it rests with me. Well, I don't like Anna Mikháylovna and I don't like Borís, but they were our friends and poor. Well then, this!" and he tore up the note, and by so doing caused the old countess to weep tears of joy. After that, young Rostóv took no further part in any business affairs, but devoted himself with passionate enthusiasm to what was to him a new pursuit—the chase—for which his father kept a large establishment.

CHAPTER III

The weather was already growing wintry and morning frosts congealed an earth saturated by autumn rains. The verdure had thickened and its bright green stood out sharply against the brownish strips of winter rye trodden down by the cattle, and against the pale-yellow stubble of the spring buckwheat. The wooded ravines and the copses, which at the end of August had still been green islands amid black fields and stubble, had become golden and bright-red islands amid the green winter rye. The hares had already half changed their summer coats, the fox cubs were beginning to scatter, and the young wolves were bigger than dogs. It was the best time of the year for the chase. The hounds of that ardent young sportsman Rostóv had not merely reached hard winter condition, but were so jaded that at a meeting of the huntsmen it was decided to give them a three days' rest and then, on the sixteenth of September, to go on a distant expedition, starting from the oak grove where there was an undisturbed litter of wolf cubs.

All that day the hounds remained at home. It was frosty and the air was sharp, but toward evening the sky became overcast and it began to thaw. On the fifteenth, when young Rostóv, in his dressing gown, looked out of the window, he saw it was an unsurpassable morning for hunting: it was as if the sky were melting and sinking to the earth without any wind. The only motion in the air was that of the dripping, microscopic particles of drizzling mist. The bare twigs in the garden were hung with transparent drops which fell on the freshly fallen leaves. The earth in the kitchen garden looked wet and black and glistened like poppy seed and at a short distance merged into the dull, moist veil of mist. Nicholas went out into the wet and muddy porch. There was a smell of decaying leaves and of dog. Mílka, a black-spotted, broad-haunched bitch with prominent black eyes, got up on seeing her master, stretched her hind legs, lay down like a hare, and then suddenly jumped up and licked him right on his nose and mustache. Another borzoi, a dog, catching sight of his master from the garden path, arched his back and, rushing headlong toward the porch with lifted tail, began rubbing himself against his legs.

"O-hoy!" came at that moment, that inimitable huntsman's call which unites the deepest bass with the shrillest tenor, and round the corner came Daniel the head huntsman and head kennelman, a gray, wrinkled old man with hair cut straight over his forehead, Ukrainian fashion, a long bent whip in his hand, and that look of independence and scorn of everything that is only seen in huntsmen. He doffed his Circassian cap to his master and looked at him scornfully. This scorn was not offensive to his master. Nicholas knew that this Daniel, disdainful of everybody and who considered himself above them, was all the same his serf and huntsman.

"Daniel!" Nicholas said timidly, conscious at the sight of the weather, the hounds, and the huntsman that he was being carried away by that irresistible passion for sport which makes a man forget all his previous resolutions, as a lover forgets in the presence of his mistress.

"What orders, your excellency?" said the huntsman in his deep bass, deep as a proto-deacon's and hoarse with hallooing—and two flashing black eyes gazed from under his brows at his master, who was silent. "Can you resist it?" those eyes seemed to be asking.

"It's a good day, eh? For a hunt and a gallop, eh?" asked Nicholas, scratching Mílka behind the ears.

Daniel did not answer, but winked instead.

"I sent Uvárka at dawn to listen," his bass boomed out after a minute's pause. "He says *she's moved them* into the Otrádnoe enclosure. They were howling there." (This meant that the she-wolf, about whom they both knew, had moved with her cubs to the Otrádnoecopse, a small place a mile and a half from the house.)

"We ought to go, don't you think so?" said Nicholas. "Come to me with Uvárka."

"As you please."

"Then put off feeding them."

"Yes, sir."

Five minutes later Daniel and Uvárka were standing in Nicholas' big study. Though Daniel was not a big man, to see him in a room was like seeing a horse or a bear on the floor among the furniture and surroundings of human life. Daniel himself felt this, and as usual stood just inside the door, trying to speak softly and not move, for fear of breaking something in the master's apartment, and he hastened to say all that was necessary so as to get from under that ceiling, out into the open under the sky once more.

Having finished his inquiries and extorted from Daniel an opinion that the hounds were fit (Daniel himself wished to go hunting), Nicholas ordered the horses to be saddled. But just as Daniel was about to go Natásha came in with rapid steps, not having done up her hair or finished dressing and with her old nurse's big shawl wrapped round her. Pétya ran in at the same time.

"You are going?" asked Natásha. "I knew you would! Sónya said you wouldn't go, but I knew that today is the sort of day when you couldn't help going."

"Yes, we are going," replied Nicholas reluctantly, for today, as he intended to hunt seriously, he did not want to take Natásha and Pétya. "We are going, but only wolf hunting: it would be dull for you."

"You know it is my greatest pleasure," said Natásha. "It's not fair; you are going by yourself, are having the horses saddled and said nothing to us about it."

"'No barrier bars a Russian's path'—we'll go!" shouted Pétya.

"But you can't. Mamma said you mustn't," said Nicholas to Natásha.

"Yes, I'll go. I shall certainly go," said Natásha decisively. "Daniel, tell them to saddle for us, and Michael must come with my dogs," she added to the huntsman.

It seemed to Daniel irksome and improper to be in a room at all, but to have anything to do with a young lady seemed to him impossible. He cast down his eyes and hurried out as if it were none of his business, careful as he went not to inflict any accidental injury on the young lady.

CHAPTER IV

The old count, who had always kept up an enormous hunting establishment but had now handed it all completely over to his son's care, being in very good spirits on this fifteenth of September, prepared to go out with the others.

In an hour's time the whole hunting party was at the porch. Nicholas, with a stern and serious air which showed that now was no time for attending to trifles, went past Natásha and Pétya who were trying to tell him something. He had a look at all the details of the hunt, sent a pack of hounds and huntsmen on ahead to find the quarry, mounted his chestnut Donéts, and whistling to his own leash of borzois, set off across the threshing ground to a field leading to the Otrádnoe wood. The old count's horse, a sorrel gelding called Viflyánka, was led by the groom in attendance on him, while the count himself was to drive in a small trap straight to a spot reserved for him.

They were taking fifty-four hounds, with six hunt attendants and whippers-in. Besides the family, there were eight borzoi kennelmen and more than forty borzois, so that, with the borzois on the leash belonging to members of the family, there were about a hundred and thirty dogs and twenty horsemen.

Each dog knew its master and its call. Each man in the hunt knew his business, his place, what he had to do. As soon as they had passed the fence they all spread out evenly and quietly, without noise or talk, along the road and field leading to the Otrádnoe covert.

The horses stepped over the field as over a thick carpet, now and then splashing into puddles as they crossed a road. The misty sky still seemed to descend evenly and imperceptibly toward the earth, the air was still, warm, and silent. Occasionally the whistle of a huntsman, the snort of a horse, the crack of a whip, or the whine of a straggling hound could be heard.

When they had gone a little less than a mile, five more riders with dogs appeared out of the mist, approaching the Rostóvs. In front rode a fresh-looking, handsome old man with a large graymustache.

"Good morning, Uncle!" said Nicholas, when the old man drew near.

"That's it. Come on!... I was sure of it," began "Uncle." (He was a distant relative of the Rostóvs', a man of small means, and their neighbor.) "I knew you wouldn't be able to resist it and it's a good thing you're going. That's it! Come on!" (This was "Uncle's" favorite expression.) "Take the covert at once, for my Gírchik says the Ilágins are at Korníkí with their hounds. That's it. Come on!... They'll take the cubs from under your very nose."

"That's where I'm going. Shall we join up our packs?" asked Nicholas.

The hounds were joined into one pack, and "Uncle" and Nicholas rode on side by side. Natásha, muffled up in shawls which did not hide her eager face and shining eyes, galloped up to them. She was followed by Pétya who always kept close to her, by Michael, a huntsman, and by a groom appointed to look after her. Pétya, who was laughing, whipped and pulled at his horse. Natásha sat easily and confidently on her black Arábchik and reined him in without effort with a firm hand.

"Uncle" looked round disapprovingly at Pétya and Natásha. He did not like to combine frivolity with the serious business of hunting.

"Good morning, Uncle! We are going too!" shouted Pétya.

"Good morning, good morning! But don't go overriding the hounds," said "Uncle" sternly.

"Nicholas, what a fine dog Truníla is! He knew me," said Natásha, referring to her favorite hound.

"In the first place, Truníla is not a 'dog,' but a harrier," thought Nicholas, and looked sternly at his sister, trying to make her feel the distance that ought to separate them at that moment. Natásha understood it.

"You mustn't think we'll be in anyone's way, Uncle," she said. "We'll go to our places and won't budge."

"A good thing too, little countess," said "Uncle," "only mind you don't fall off your horse," he added, "because—that's it, come on!—you've nothing to hold on to."

The oasis of the Otrádnoe covert came in sight a few hundred yards off, the huntsmen were already nearing it. Rostóv, having finally settled with "Uncle" where they should set on the hounds, and having shown Natásha where she was to stand—a spot where nothing could possibly run out—went round above the ravine.

"Well, nephew, you're going for a big wolf," said "Uncle." "Mind and don't let her slip!"

"That's as may happen," answered Rostóv. "Karáy, here!" he shouted, answering "Uncle's" remark by this call to his borzoi. Karáy was a shaggy old dog with a hanging jowl, famous for having tackled a big wolf unaided. They all took up their places.

The old count, knowing his son's ardor in the hunt, hurried so as not to be late, and the huntsmen had not yet reached their places when Count IlyáRostóv, cheerful, flushed, and with quivering cheeks, drove up with his black horses over the winter rye to the place reserved for him, where a wolf might come out. Having straightened his coat and fastened on his hunting knives and horn, he mounted his good, sleek, well-fed, and comfortable horse, Viflyánka, which was turning gray, like himself. His horses and trap were sent home. Count IlyáRostóv, though not at heart a keen sportsman, knew the rules of the hunt well, and rode to the bushy edge of the road where he was to stand, arranged his reins, settled himself in the saddle, and, feeling that he was ready, looked about with a smile.

Beside him was Simon Chekmár, his personal attendant, an old horseman now somewhat stiff in the saddle. Chekmár held in leash three formidable wolfhounds, who had, however, grown fat like their master and his horse. Two wise old dogs lay down unleashed. Some hundred paces farther along the edge of the wood stood Mítka, the count's other groom, a daring horseman and keen rider to hounds. Before the hunt, by old custom, the count had drunk a silver cupful of mulled brandy, taken a snack, and washed it down with half a bottle of his favorite Bordeaux.

He was somewhat flushed with the wine and the drive. His eyes were rather moist and glittered more than usual, and as he sat in his saddle, wrapped up in his fur coat, he looked like a child taken out for an outing.

The thin, hollow-cheeked Chekmár, having got everything ready, kept glancing at his master with whom he had lived on the best of terms for thirty years, and understanding the mood he was in expected a pleasant chat. A third person rode up circumspectly through the wood (it was plain that he had had a lesson) and stopped behind the count. This person was a gray-bearded old man in a woman's cloak, with a tall peaked cap on his head. He was the buffoon, who went by a woman's name, NastásyaIvánovna.

"Well, NastásyaIvánovna!" whispered the count, winking at him. "If you scare away the beast, Daniel'll give it you!"

"I know a thing or two myself!" said NastásyaIvánovna.

"Hush!" whispered the count and turned to Simon. "Have you seen the young countess?" he asked. "Where is she?"

"With young Count Peter, by the Zhárov rank grass," answered Simon, smiling. "Though she's a lady, she's very fond of hunting."

"And you're surprised at the way she rides, Simon, eh?" said the count. "She's as good as many a man!"

"Of course! It's marvelous. So bold, so easy!"

"And Nicholas? Where is he? By the Lyádov upland, isn't he?"

"Yes, sir. He knows where to stand. He understands the matter so well that Daniel and I are often quite astounded," said Simon, well knowing what would please his master.

"Rides well, eh? And how well he looks on his horse, eh?"

"A perfect picture! How he chased a fox out of the rank grass by the Zavárzinsk thicket the other day! Leaped a fearful place; what a sight when they rushed from the covert... the horse worth a thousand rubles and the rider beyond all price! Yes, one would have to search far to find another as smart."

"'To search far..." repeated the count, evidently sorry Simon had not said more. "To search far," he said, turning back the skirt of his coat to get at his snuffbox.

"The other day when he came out from Mass in full uniform, Michael Sidórych..." Simon did not finish, for on the still air he had distinctly caught the music of the hunt with only two or three hounds giving tongue. He bent down his head and listened, shaking a warning finger at his master. "They are on the scent of the cubs..." he whispered, "straight to the Lyádov uplands."

The count, forgetting to smooth out the smile on his face, looked into the distance straight before him, down the narrow open space, holding the snuffbox in his hand but not taking any. After the cry of the hounds came the deep tones of the wolf call from Daniel's hunting horn; the pack joined the first three hounds and they could be heard in full cry, with that peculiar lift in the note that indicates that they are after a wolf. The whippers-in no longer set on the hounds, but changed to the cry of *ulyulyu*, and above the others rose Daniel's voice, now a deep bass, now piercingly shrill. His voice seemed to fill the whole wood and carried far beyond out into the open field.

After listening a few moments in silence, the count and his attendant convinced themselves that the hounds had separated into two packs: the sound of the larger pack, eagerly giving tongue, began to die away in the distance, the other pack rushed by the wood past the count, and it was with this that Daniel's voice was heard calling *ulyulyu*. The sounds of both packs mingled and broke apart again, but both were becoming more distant.

Simon sighed and stooped to straighten the leash a young borzoi had entangled; the count too sighed and, noticing the snuffbox in his hand, opened it and took a pinch. "Back!" cried Simon to a borzoi that was pushing forward out of the wood. The count started and dropped the snuffbox. Nastásyalvánovna dismounted to pick it up. The count and Simon were looking at him.

Then, unexpectedly, as often happens, the sound of the hunt suddenly approached, as if the hounds in full cry and Daniel *ulyulyuing* were just in front of them.

The count turned and saw on his right Mítka staring at him with eyes starting out of his head, raising his cap and pointing before him to the other side.

"Look out!" he shouted, in a voice plainly showing that he had long fretted to utter that word, and letting the borzois slip he galloped toward the count.

The count and Simon galloped out of the wood and saw on their left a wolf which, softly swaying from side to side, was coming at a quiet lope farther to the left to the very place where they were standing. The angry borzois whined and getting free of the leash rushed past the horses' feet at the wolf.

The wolf paused, turned its heavy forehead toward the dogs awkwardly, like a man suffering from the quinsy, and, still slightly swaying from side to side, gave a couple of leaps and with a swish of its tail disappeared into the skirt of the wood. At the same instant, with a cry like a wail, first one hound, then another, and then another, sprang helter-skelter from the wood opposite and the whole pack rushed across the field toward the very spot where the wolf had disappeared. The hazel bushes parted behind the hounds and Daniel's chestnut horse appeared, dark with sweat. On its long back sat Daniel, hunched forward, capless, his disheveledgray hair hanging over his flushed, perspiring face.

"*Ulyulyulyu! ulyulyu!...*" he cried. When he caught sight of the count his eyes flashed lightning.

"Blast you!" he shouted, holding up his whip threateningly at the count.

"You've let the wolf go!... What sportsmen!" and as if scorning to say more to the frightened and shamefaced count, he lashed the heaving flanks of his sweating chestnut gelding with all the anger the count had aroused and flew off after the hounds. The count, like a punished schoolboy, looked round, trying by a smile to win Simon's sympathy for his plight. But Simon was no longer there. He was galloping round by the bushes while the field was coming up on both sides, all trying to head the wolf, but it vanished into the wood before they could do so.

CHAPTER V

Nicholas Rostóv meanwhile remained at his post, waiting for the wolf. By the way the hunt approached and receded, by the cries of the dogs whose notes were familiar to him, by the way the voices of the huntsmen approached, receded, and rose, he realized what was happening at the copse. He knew that young and old wolves were there, that the hounds had separated into two packs, that somewhere a wolf was being chased, and that something had gone wrong. He expected the wolf to come his way any moment. He made thousands of different conjectures as to where and from what side the beast would come and how he would set upon it. Hope alternated with despair. Several times he addressed a prayer to God that the wolf should come his way. He prayed with that passionate and shamefaced feeling with which men pray at moments of great excitement arising from trivial causes. "What would it be to Thee to do this for me?" he said to God. "I know Thou art great, and that it is a sin to ask this of Thee, but for God's sake do let the old wolf come my way and let Karáy spring at it—in sight of 'Uncle' who is watching from over there—and seize it by the throat in a death grip!" A thousand times during that half-hour Rostóv cast eager and restless glances over the edge of the wood, with the two scraggy oaks rising above the aspen undergrowth and the gully with its water-worn side and "Uncle's" cap just visible above the bush on his right.

"No, I shan't have such luck," thought Rostóv, "yet what wouldn't it be worth! It is not to be! Everywhere, at cards and in war, I am always unlucky." Memories of Austerlitz and of Dólokhov flashed rapidly and clearly through his mind. "Only once in my life to get an old wolf, I want only that!" thought he, straining eyes and ears and looking to the left and then to the right and listening to the slightest variation of note in the cries of the dogs.

Again he looked to the right and saw something running toward him across the deserted field. "No, it can't be!" thought Rostóv, taking a deep breath, as a man does at the coming of something long hoped for. The height of happiness was reached—and so simply, without warning, or noise, or display, that Rostóv could not believe his eyes and remained in doubt for over a second. The wolf ran forward and jumped heavily over a gully that lay in her path. She was an old animal with a gray back and big reddish belly. She ran without hurry, evidently feeling sure that no one saw her. Rostóv, holding his breath, looked round at the borzois. They stood or lay not seeing the wolf or understanding the situation. Old Karáy had turned his head and was angrily searching for fleas, baring his yellow teeth and snapping at his hind legs.

"Ulyulyulyu!" whispered Rostóv, pouting his lips. The borzois jumped up, jerking the rings of the leashes and pricking their ears. Karáy finished scratching his hindquarters and, cocking his ears, got up with quivering tail from which tufts of matted hair hung down.

"Shall I loose them or not?" Nicholas asked himself as the wolf approached him coming from the copse. Suddenly the wolf's whole physiognomy changed: she shuddered, seeing what she had probably never seen before—human eyes fixed upon her—and turning her head a little toward Rostóv, she paused.

"Back or forward? Eh, no matter, forward..." the wolf seemed to say to herself, and she moved forward without again looking round and with a quiet, long, easy yet resolute lope.

"Ulyulyu!" cried Nicholas, in a voice not his own, and of its own accord his good horse darted headlong downhill, leaping over gullies to head off the wolf, and the borzois passed it, running faster still. Nicholas did not hear his own cry nor feel that he was galloping, nor see the borzois, nor the ground over which he went: he saw only the wolf, who, increasing her speed, bounded on in the same direction along the hollow. The first to come into view was Mílka, with her black markings and powerful quarters, gaining upon the wolf. Nearer and nearer... now she was ahead of it; but the wolf turned its head to face her, and instead of putting on speed as she usually did Mílka suddenly raised her tail and stiffened her forelegs.

"Ulyulyulyulyu!" shouted Nicholas.

The reddish Lyubím rushed forward from behind Mílka, sprang impetuously at the wolf, and seized it by its hindquarters, but immediately jumped aside in terror. The wolf crouched, gnashed her teeth, and again rose and bounded forward, followed at the distance of a couple of feet by all the borzois, who did not get any closer to her.

"She'll get away! No, it's impossible!" thought Nicholas, still shouting with a hoarse voice.

"Karáy, *ulyulyu!...*" he shouted, looking round for the old borzoi who was now his only hope. Karáy, with all the strength age had left him, stretched himself to the utmost and, watching the wolf, galloped heavily aside to intercept it. But the quickness of the wolf's lope and the borzoi's slower pace made it plain that Karáy had miscalculated. Nicholas could already see not far in front of him the wood where the wolf would certainly escape should she reach it. But, coming toward him, he saw hounds and a huntsman galloping almost straight at the wolf. There was still hope. A long, yellowish young borzoi, one Nicholas did not know, from another leash, rushed impetuously at the wolf from in front and almost knocked her over. But the wolf jumped up more quickly than anyone could have expected and, gnashing her teeth, flew at the yellowish borzoi, which, with a piercing yelp, fell with its head on the ground, bleeding from a gash in its side.

"Karáy? Old fellow!..." wailed Nicholas.

Thanks to the delay caused by this crossing of the wolf's path, the old dog with its felted hair hanging from its thigh was within five paces of it. As if aware of her danger, the wolf turned her eyes on Karáy, tucked her tail yet further between her legs, and increased her speed. But here Nicholas only saw that something happened to Karáy—the borzoi was suddenly on the wolf, and they rolled together down into a gully just in front of them.

That instant, when Nicholas saw the wolf struggling in the gully with the dogs, while from under them could be seen her gray hair and outstretched hind leg and her frightened choking head, with her ears laid back (Karáy was pinning her by the throat), was the happiest moment of his life. With his hand on his saddlebow, he was ready to dismount and stab the wolf, when she suddenly thrust her head up from among that mass of dogs, and then her forepaws were on the edge of the gully. She clicked her teeth (Karáy no longer had her by the throat), leaped with a movement of her hind legs out of the gully, and having disengaged herself from the dogs, with tail tucked in again, went forward. Karáy, his hair bristling, and probably bruised or wounded, climbed with difficulty out of the gully.

"Oh my God! Why?" Nicholas cried in despair.

"Uncle's" huntsman was galloping from the other side across the wolf's path and his borzois once more stopped the animal's advance. She was again hemmed in.

Nicholas and his attendant, with "Uncle" and his huntsman, were all riding round the wolf, crying *"ulyulyu!"* shouting and preparing to dismount each moment that the wolf crouched back, and starting forward again every time she shook herself and moved toward the wood where she would be safe.

Already, at the beginning of this chase, Daniel, hearing the ulyulyuing, had rushed out from the wood. He saw Karáy seize the wolf, and checked his horse, supposing the affair to be over. But when he saw that the horsemen did not dismount and that the wolf shook herself and ran for safety, Daniel set his chestnut galloping, not at the wolf but straight toward the wood, just as Karáy had run to cut the animal off. As a result of this, he galloped up to the wolf just when she had been stopped a second time by "Uncle's" borzois.

Daniel galloped up silently, holding a naked dagger in his left hand and thrashing the laboring sides of his chestnut horse with his whip as if it were a flail.

Nicholas neither saw nor heard Daniel until the chestnut, breathing heavily, panted past him, and he heard the fall of a body and saw Daniel lying on the wolf's back among the dogs, trying to seize her by the ears. It was evident to the dogs, the hunters, and to the wolf herself that all was now over. The terrified wolf pressed back her ears and tried to rise, but the borzois stuck to her. Daniel rose a little, took a step, and with his whole weight, as if lying down to rest, fell on the wolf, seizing her by the ears. Nicholas was about to stab her, but Daniel whispered, "Don't! We'll gag her!" and, changing his position, set his foot on the wolf's neck. A stick was thrust between her jaws and she was fastened with a leash, as if bridled, her legs were bound together, and Daniel rolled her over once or twice from side to side.

With happy, exhausted faces, they laid the old wolf, alive, on a shying and snorting horse and, accompanied by the dogs yelping at her, took her to the place where they were all to meet. The hounds had killed two of the cubs and the borzois three. The huntsmen assembled with their booty and their stories, and all came to look at the wolf, which, with her broad-browed head hanging down and the bitten stick between her jaws, gazed with great glassy eyes at this crowd of dogs and men surrounding her. When she was touched, she jerked her bound legs and looked wildly yet simply at everybody. Old Count Rostóv also rode up and touched the wolf.

"Oh, what a formidable one!" said he. "A formidable one, eh?" he asked Daniel, who was standing near.

"Yes, your excellency," answered Daniel, quickly doffing his cap.

The count remembered the wolf he had let slip and his encounter with Daniel.

"Ah, but you are a crusty fellow, friend!" said the count.

For sole reply Daniel gave him a shy, childlike, meek, and amiable smile.

CHAPTER VI

The old count went home, and Natásha and Pétya promised to return very soon, but as it was still early the hunt went farther. At midday they put the hounds into a ravine thickly overgrown with young trees. Nicholas standing in a fallow field could see all his whips.

Facing him lay a field of winter rye, there his own huntsman stood alone in a hollow behind a hazel bush. The hounds had scarcely been loosed before Nicholas heard one he knew, Voltórn, giving tongue at intervals; other hounds joined in, now pausing and now again giving tongue. A moment later he heard a cry from the wooded ravine that a fox had been found, and the whole pack, joining together, rushed along the ravine toward the ryefield and away from Nicholas.

He saw the whips in their red caps galloping along the edge of the ravine, he even saw the hounds, and was expecting a fox to show itself at any moment on the ryefield opposite.

The huntsman standing in the hollow moved and loosed his borzois, and Nicholas saw a queer, short-legged red fox with a fine brush going hard across the field. The borzois bore down on it.... Now they drew close to the fox which began to dodge between the field in sharper and sharper curves, trailing its brush, when suddenly a strange white borzoi dashed in followed by a black one, and everything was in confusion; the borzois formed a star-shaped figure, scarcely swaying their bodies and with tails turned away from the center of the group. Two huntsmen galloped up to the dogs; one in a red cap, the other, a stranger, in a green coat.

"What's this?" thought Nicholas. "Where's that huntsman from? He is not 'Uncle's' man."

The huntsmen got the fox, but stayed there a long time without strapping it to the saddle. Their horses, bridled and with high saddles, stood near them and there too the dogs were lying. The huntsmen waved their arms and did something to the fox. Then from that spot came the sound of a horn, with the signal agreed on in case of a fight.

"That's Ilágin's huntsman having a row with our Iván," said Nicholas' groom.

Nicholas sent the man to call Natásha and Pétya to him, and rode at a footpace to the place where the whips were getting the hounds together. Several of the field galloped to the spot where the fight was going on.

Nicholas dismounted, and with Natásha and Pétya, who had ridden up, stopped near the hounds, waiting to see how the matter would end. Out of the bushes came the huntsman who had been fighting and rode toward his young master, with the fox tied to his crupper. While still at a distance he took off his cap and tried to speak respectfully, but he was pale and breathless and his face was angry. One of his eyes was black, but he probably was not even aware of it.

"What has happened?" asked Nicholas.

"A likely thing, killing a fox our dogs had hunted! And it was my gray bitch that caught it! Go to law, indeed!... He snatches at the fox! I gave him one with the fox. Here it is on my saddle! Do you want a taste of this?..." said the huntsman, pointing to his dagger and probably imagining himself still speaking to his foe.

Nicholas, not stopping to talk to the man, asked his sister and Pétya to wait for him and rode to the spot where the enemy's, Ilágin's, hunting party was.

The victorious huntsman rode off to join the field, and there, surrounded by inquiring sympathizers, recounted his exploits.

The facts were that Ilágin, with whom the Rostóvs had a quarrel and were at law, hunted over places that belonged by custom to the Rostóvs, and had now, as if purposely, sent his men to the very woods the Rostóvs were hunting and let his man snatch a fox their dogs had chased.

Nicholas, though he had never seen Ilágin, with his usual absence of moderation in judgment, hated him cordially from reports of his arbitrariness and violence, and regarded him as his bitterest foe. He rode in angry agitation toward him, firmly grasping his whip and fully prepared to take the most resolute and desperate steps to punish his enemy.

Hardly had he passed an angle of the wood before a stout gentleman in a beaver cap came riding toward him on a handsome raven-black horse, accompanied by two hunt servants.

Instead of an enemy, Nicholas found in Ilágin a stately and courteous gentleman who was particularly anxious to make the young count's acquaintance. Having ridden up to Nicholas, Ilágin raised his beaver cap and said he much regretted what had occurred and would have the man punished who had allowed himself to seize a fox hunted by someone else's borzois. He hoped to become better acquainted with the count and invited him to draw his covert.

Natásha, afraid that her brother would do something dreadful, had followed him in some excitement. Seeing the enemies exchanging friendly greetings, she rode up to them. Ilágin lifted his beaver cap still higher to Natásha and said, with a pleasant smile, that the young countess resembled Diana in her passion for the chase as well as in her beauty, of which he had heard much.

To expiate his huntsman's offense, Ilágin pressed the Rostóvs to come to an upland of his about a mile away which he usually kept for himself and which, he said, swarmed with hares. Nicholas agreed, and the hunt, now doubled, moved on.

The way to Iligin's upland was across the fields. The hunt servants fell into line. The masters rode together. "Uncle," Rostóv, and Ilágin kept stealthily glancing at one another's dogs, trying not to be observed by their companions and searching uneasily for rivals to their own borzois.

Rostóv was particularly struck by the beauty of a small, pure-bred, red-spotted bitch on Ilágin's leash, slender but with muscles like steel, a delicate muzzle, and prominent black eyes. He had heard of the swiftness of Ilágin's borzois, and in that beautiful bitch saw a rival to his own Mílka.

In the middle of a sober conversation begun by Ilágin about the year's harvest, Nicholas pointed to the red-spotted bitch.

"A fine little bitch, that!" said he in a careless tone. "Is she swift?"

"That one? Yes, she's a good dog, gets what she's after," answered Ilágin indifferently, of the red-spotted bitch Erzá, for which, a year before, he had given a neighbor three families of house serfs. "So in your parts, too, the harvest is nothing to boast of, Count?" he went on, continuing the conversation they had begun. And considering it polite to return the young count's compliment, Ilágin looked at his borzois and picked out Mílka who attracted his attention by her breadth. "That black-spotted one of yours is fine—well shaped!" said he.

"Yes, she's fast enough," replied Nicholas, and thought: "If only a full-grown hare would cross the field now I'd show you what sort of borzoi she is," and turning to his groom, he said he would give a ruble to anyone who found a hare.

"I don't understand," continued Ilágin, "how some sportsmen can be so jealous about game and dogs. For myself, I can tell you, Count, I enjoy riding in company such as this... what could be better?" (he again raised his cap to Natásha) "but as for counting skins and what one takes, I don't care about that."

"Of course not!"

"Or being upset because someone else's borzoi and not mine catches something. All I care about is to enjoy seeing the chase, is it not so, Count? For I consider that..."

"*A-tu!*" came the long-drawn cry of one of the borzoi whippers-in, who had halted. He stood on a knoll in the stubble, holding his whip aloft, and again repeated his long-drawn cry, "*A-tu!*" (This call and the uplifted whip meant that he saw a sitting hare.)

"Ah, he has found one, I think," said Ilágin carelessly. "Yes, we must ride up.... Shall we both course it?" answered Nicholas, seeing in Erzá and "Uncle's" red Rugáy two rivals he had never yet had a chance of pitting against his own borzois. "And suppose they outdo my Mílka at once!" he thought as he rode with "Uncle" and Ilágin toward the hare.

"A full-grown one?" asked Ilágin as he approached the whip who had sighted the hare—and not without agitation he looked round and whistled to Erzá.

"And you, Michael Nikanórovich?" he said, addressing "Uncle."

The latter was riding with a sullen expression on his face.

"How can I join in? Why, you've given a village for each of your borzois! That's it, come on! Yours are worth thousands. Try yours against one another, you two, and I'll look on!"

"Rugáy, hey, hey!" he shouted. "Rugáyushka!" he added, involuntarily by this diminutive expressing his affection and the hopes he placed on this red borzoi. Natásha saw and felt the agitation the two elderly men and her brother were trying to conceal, and was herself excited by it.

The huntsman stood halfway up the knoll holding up his whip and the gentlefolk rode up to him at a footpace; the hounds that were far off on the horizon turned away from the hare, and the whips, but not the gentlefolk, also moved away. All were moving slowly and sedately.

"How is it pointing?" asked Nicholas, riding a hundred paces toward the whip who had sighted the hare.

But before the whip could reply, the hare, scenting the frost coming next morning, was unable to rest and leaped up. The pack on leash rushed downhill in full cry after the hare, and from all sides the borzois that were not on leash darted after the hounds and the hare. All the hunt, who had been moving slowly, shouted, "Stop!" calling in the hounds, while the borzoi whips, with a cry of "A-tu!" galloped across the field setting the borzois on the hare. The tranquil Ilágin, Nicholas, Natásha, and "Uncle" flew, reckless of where and how they went, seeing only the borzois and the hare and fearing only to lose sight even for an instant of the chase. The hare they had started was a strong and swift one. When he jumped up he did not run at once, but pricked his ears listening to the shouting and trampling that resounded from all sides at once. He took a dozen bounds, not very quickly, letting the borzois gain on him, and, finally having chosen his direction and realized his danger, laid back his ears and rushed off headlong. He had been lying in the stubble, but in front of him was the autumn sowing where the ground was soft. The two borzois of the huntsman who had sighted him, having been the nearest, were the first to see and pursue him, but they had not gone far before Ilágin's red-spotted Erzá passed them, got within a length, flew at the hare with terrible swiftness aiming at his scut, and, thinking she had seized him, rolled over like a ball. The hare arched his back and bounded off yet more swiftly. From behind Erzá rushed the broad-haunched, black-spotted Mílka and began rapidly gaining on the hare.

"Miláshka, dear!" rose Nicholas' triumphant cry. It looked as if Mílka would immediately pounce on the hare, but she overtook him and flew past. The hare had squatted. Again the beautiful Erzá reached him, but when close to the hare's scut paused as if measuring the distance, so as not to make a mistake this time but seize his hind leg.

"Erzá, darling!" Ilágin wailed in a voice unlike his own. Erzá did not hearken to his appeal. At the very moment when she would have seized her prey, the hare moved and darted along the balk between the winter rye and the stubble. AgainErzá and Mílka were abreast, running like a pair of carriage horses, and began to overtake the hare, but it was easier for the hare to run on the balk and the borzois did not overtake him so quickly.

"Rugáy, Rugáyushka! That's it, come on!" came a third voice just then, and "Uncle's" red borzoi, straining and curving its back, caught up with the two foremost borzois, pushed ahead of them regardless of the terrible strain, put on speed close to the hare, knocked it off the balk onto the ryefield, again put on speed still more viciously, sinking to his knees in the muddy field, and all one could see was how, muddying his back, he rolled over with the hare. A ring of borzois surrounded him. A moment later everyone had drawn up round the crowd of dogs. Only the delighted "Uncle" dismounted, and cut off a pad, shaking the hare for the blood to drip off, and anxiously glancing round with restless eyes while his arms and legs twitched. He spoke without himself knowing whom to or what about. "That's it, come on! That's a dog!... There, it has beaten them all, the thousand-ruble as well as the one-ruble borzois. That's it, come on!" said he, panting and looking wrathfully around as if he were abusing someone, as if they were all his enemies and had insulted him, and only now had he at last succeeded in justifying himself. "There are your thousand-ruble ones.... That's it, come on!..."

"Rugáy, here's a pad for you!" he said, throwing down the hare's muddy pad. "You've deserved it, that's it, come on!"

"She'd tired herself out, she'd run it down three times by herself," said Nicholas, also not listening to anyone and regardless of whether he were heard or not.

"But what is there in running across it like that?" said Ilágin's groom.

"Once she had missed it and turned it away, any mongrel could take it," Ilágin was saying at the same time, breathless from his gallop and his excitement. At the same moment Natásha, without drawing breath, screamed joyously, ecstatically, and so piercingly that it set everyone's ear tingling. By that shriek she expressed what the others expressed by all talking at once, and it was so strange that she must herself have been ashamed of so wild a cry and everyone else would have been amazed at it at any other time. "Uncle" himself twisted up the hare, threw it neatly and smartly across his horse's back as if by that gesture he meant to rebuke everybody, and, with an air of not wishing to speak to anyone, mounted his bay and rode off. The others all followed, dispirited and shamefaced, and only much later were they able to regain their former affectation of indifference. For a long time they continued to look at red Rugáy who, his arched back spattered with mud and clanking the ring of his leash, walked along just behind "Uncle's" horse with the serene air of a conqueror.

"Well, I am like any other dog as long as it's not a question of coursing. But when it is, then look out!" his appearance seemed to Nicholas to be saying.

When, much later, "Uncle" rode up to Nicholas and began talking to him, he felt flattered that, after what had happened, "Uncle" deigned to speak to him.

CHAPTER VII

Toward evening Ilágin took leave of Nicholas, who found that they were so far from home that he accepted "Uncle's" offer that the hunting party should spend the night in his little village of Mikháylovna.

"And if you put up at my house that will be better still. That's it, come on!" said "Uncle." "You see it's damp weather, and you could rest, and the little countess could be driven home in a trap."

"Uncle's" offer was accepted. A huntsman was sent to Otrádnoe for a trap, while Nicholas rode with Natásha and Pétya to "Uncle's" house.

Some five male domestic serfs, big and little, rushed out to the front porch to meet their master. A score of women serfs, old and young, as well as children, popped out from the back entrance to have a look at the hunters who were arriving. The presence of Natásha—a woman, a lady, and on horseback—raised the curiosity of the serfs to such a degree that many of them came up to her, stared her in the face, and unabashed by her presence made remarks about her as though she were some prodigy on show and not a human being able to hear or understand what was said about her.

"Arínka! Look, she sits sideways! There she sits and her skirt dangles.... See, she's got a little hunting horn!"

"Goodness gracious! See her knife?..."

"Isn't she a Tartar!"

"How is it you didn't go head over heels?" asked the boldest of all, addressing Natásha directly.

"Uncle" dismounted at the porch of his little wooden house which stood in the midst of an overgrown garden and, after a glance at his retainers, shouted authoritatively that the superfluous ones should take themselves off and that all necessary preparations should be made to receive the guests and the visitors.

The serfs all dispersed. "Uncle" lifted Natásha off her horse and taking her hand led her up the rickety wooden steps of the porch. The house, with its bare, unplastered log walls, was not overclean—it did not seem that those living in it aimed at keeping it spotless—but neither was it noticeably neglected. In the entry there was a smell of fresh apples, and wolf and fox skins hung about.

"Uncle" led the visitors through the anteroom into a small hall with a folding table and red chairs, then into the drawing room with a round birchwood table and a sofa, and finally into his private room where there was a tattered sofa, a worn carpet, and portraits of Suvórov, of the host's father and mother, and of himself in military uniform. The study smelt strongly of tobacco and dogs. "Uncle" asked his visitors to sit down and make themselves at home, and then went out of the room. Rugáy, his back still muddy, came into the room and lay down on the sofa, cleaning himself with his tongue and teeth. Leading from the study was a passage in which a partition with ragged curtains could be seen. From behind this came women's laughter and whispers. Natásha, Nicholas, and Pétya took off their wraps and sat down on the sofa. Pétya, leaning on his elbow, fell asleep at once. Natásha and Nicholas were silent. Their faces glowed, they were hungry and very cheerful. They looked at one another (now that the hunt was over and they were in the house, Nicholas no longer considered it necessary to show his manly superiority over his sister), Natásha gave him a wink, and neither refrained long from bursting into a peal of ringing laughter even before they had a pretext ready to account for it.

After a while "Uncle" came in, in a Cossack coat, blue trousers, and small top boots. And Natásha felt that this costume, the very one she had regarded with surprise and amusement at Otrádnoe, was just the right thing and not at all worse than a swallow-tail or frock coat. "Uncle" too was in high spirits and far from being offended by the brother's and sister's laughter (it could never enter his head that they might be laughing at his way of life) he himself joined in the merriment.

"That's right, young countess, that's it, come on! I never saw anyone like her!" said he, offering Nicholas a pipe with a long stem and, with a practiced motion of three fingers, taking down another that had been cut short. "She's ridden all day like a man, and is as fresh as ever!"

Soon after "Uncle's" reappearance the door was opened, evidently from the sound by a barefooted girl, and a stout, rosy, good-looking woman of about forty, with a double chin and full red lips, entered carrying a large loaded tray. With hospitable dignity and cordiality in her glance and in every motion, she looked at the visitors and, with a pleasant smile, bowed respectfully. In spite of her exceptional stoutness, which caused her to protrude her chest and stomach and throw back her head, this woman (who was "Uncle's" housekeeper) trod very lightly. She went to the table, set down the tray, and with her plump white hands deftly took from it the bottles and various hors d'oeuvres and dishes and arranged them on the table. When she had finished, she stepped aside and stopped at the door with a smile on her face. "Here I am. I am she! Now do you understand 'Uncle'?" her expression said to Rostóv. How could one help understanding? Not only Nicholas, but even Natásha understood the meaning of his puckered brow and the happy complacent smile that slightly puckered his lips when AnísyaFëdorovna entered. On the tray was a bottle of herb wine, different kinds of vodka, pickled mushrooms, rye cakes made with buttermilk, honey in the comb, still mead and sparkling mead, apples, nuts (raw and roasted), and nut-and-honey sweets. Afterwards she brought a freshly roasted chicken, ham, preserves made with honey, and preserves made with sugar.

All this was the fruit of AnísyaFëdorovna's housekeeping, gathered and prepared by her. The smell and taste of it all had a smack of AnísyaFëdorovna herself: a savor of juiciness, cleanliness, whiteness, and pleasant smiles.

"Take this, little Lady-Countess!" she kept saying, as she offered Natásha first one thing and then another.

Natásha ate of everything and thought she had never seen or eaten such buttermilk cakes, such aromatic jam, such honey-and-nut sweets, or such a chicken anywhere. AnísyaFëdorovna left the room.

After supper, over their cherry brandy, Rostóv and "Uncle" talked of past and future hunts, of Rugáy and Ilágin's dogs, while

Natásha sat upright on the sofa and listened with sparkling eyes. She tried several times to wake Pétya that he might eat something, but he only muttered incoherent words without waking up. Natásha felt so lighthearted and happy in these novel surroundings that she only feared the trap would come for her too soon. After a casual pause, such as often occurs when receiving friends for the first time in one's own house, "Uncle," answering a thought that was in his visitors' minds, said:

"This, you see, is how I am finishing my days... Death will come. That's it, come on! Nothing will remain. Then why harm anyone?"

"Uncle's" face was very significant and even handsome as he said this. Involuntarily Rostóv recalled all the good he had heard about him from his father and the neighbors. Throughout the whole province "Uncle" had the reputation of being the most honorable and disinterested of cranks. They called him in to decide family disputes, chose him as executor, confided secrets to him, elected him to be a justice and to other posts; but he always persistently refused public appointments, passing the autumn and spring in the fields on his bay gelding, sitting at home in winter, and lying in his overgrown garden in summer.

"Why don't you enter the service, Uncle?"

"I did once, but gave it up. I am not fit for it. That's it, come on! I can't make head or tail of it. That's for you—I haven't brains enough. Now, hunting is another matter—that's it, come on! Open the door, there!" he shouted. "Why have you shut it?"

The door at the end of the passage led to the huntsmen's room, as they called the room for the hunt servants.

There was a rapid patter of bare feet, and an unseen hand opened the door into the huntsmen's room, from which came the clear sounds of a balaláyka on which someone, who was evidently a master of the art, was playing. Natásha had been listening to those strains for some time and now went out into the passage to hear better.

"That's Mítka, my coachman.... I have got him a good balaláyka. I'm fond of it," said "Uncle."

It was the custom for Mítka to play the balaláyka in the huntsmen's room when "Uncle" returned from the chase. "Uncle" was fond of such music.

"How good! Really very good!" said Nicholas with some unintentional superciliousness, as if ashamed to confess that the sounds pleased him very much.

"Very good?" said Natásha reproachfully, noticing her brother's tone. "Not 'very good'—it's simply delicious!"

Just as "Uncle's" pickled mushrooms, honey, and cherry brandy had seemed to her the best in the world, so also that song, at that moment, seemed to her the acme of musical delight.

"More, please, more!" cried Natásha at the door as soon as the balaláyka ceased. Mítka tuned up afresh, and recommenced thrumming the balaláyka to the air of *My Lady*, with trills and variations. "Uncle" sat listening, slightly smiling, with his head on one side. The air was repeated a hundred times. The balaláyka was retuned several times and the same notes were thrummed again, but the listeners did not grow weary of it and wished to hear it again and again. AnísyaFëdorovna came in and leaned her portly person against the doorpost.

"You like listening?" she said to Natásha, with a smile extremely like "Uncle's." "That's a good player of ours," she added.

"He doesn't play that part right!" said "Uncle" suddenly, with an energetic gesture. "Here he ought to burst out—that's it, come on!—ought to burst out."

"Do you play then?" asked Natásha.

"Uncle" did not answer, but smiled.

"Anísya, go and see if the strings of my guitar are all right. I haven't touched it for a long time. That's it—come on! I've given it up."

AnísyaFëdorovna, with her light step, willingly went to fulfill her errand and brought back the guitar.

Withoutlookingatanyone, "Uncle" blewthedustoffitand, tapping the case with his bony fingers, tuned the guitar and settled himself in his armchair. He took the guitar a little above the fingerboard, arching his left elbow with a somewhat theatrical gesture, and, with a wink at AnísyaFëdorovna, struck a single chord, pure and sonorous, and then quietly, smoothly, and confidently began playing in very slow time, not *My Lady*, but the well-known song: *Came a maiden down the street*. The tune, played with precision and in exact time, began to thrill in the hearts of Nicholas and Natásha, arousing in them the same kind of sober mirth as radiated from AnísyaFëdorovna's whole being. AnísyaFëdorovnaflushed, and drawing her kerchief over her face went laughing out of the room. "Uncle" continued to play correctly, carefully, with energetic firmness, looking with a changed and inspired expression at the spot where AnísyaFëdorovna had just stood. Something seemed to be laughing a little on one side of his face under his graymustaches, especially as the song grew brisker and the time quicker and when, here and there, as he ran his fingers over the strings, something seemed to snap.

"Lovely, lovely! Go on, Uncle, go on!" shouted Natásha as soon as he had finished. She jumped up and hugged and kissed him. "Nicholas, Nicholas!" she said, turning to her brother, as if asking him: "What is it moves me so?"

Nicholas too was greatly pleased by "Uncle's" playing, and "Uncle" played the piece over again. AnísyaFëdorovna's smiling face reappeared in the doorway and behind hers other faces...

Fetching water clear and sweet, Stop, dear maiden, I entreat—

played "Uncle" once more, running his fingers skillfully over the strings, and then he stopped short and jerked his shoulders.

"Go on, Uncle dear," Natásha wailed in an imploring tone as if her life depended on it.

"Uncle" rose, and it was as if there were two men in him: one of them smiled seriously at the merry fellow, while the merry fellow struck a naïve and precise attitude preparatory to a folk dance.

"Now then, niece!" he exclaimed, waving to Natásha the hand that had just struck a chord.

Natásha threw off the shawl from her shoulders, ran forward to face "Uncle," and setting her arms akimbo also made a motion with her shoulders and struck an attitude.

Where, how, and when had this young countess, educated by an *émigrée* French governess, imbibed from the Russian air she breathed that spirit and obtained that manner which the *pas de châle* * would, one would have supposed, long ago have effaced? But the spirit and the movements were those inimitable and unteachable Russian ones that "Uncle" had expected of her. As soon as she had struck her pose, and smiled triumphantly, proudly, and with sly merriment, the fear that had at first seized Nicholas and the others that she might not do the right thing was at an end, and they were already admiring her.

* The French shawl dance.

She did the right thing with such precision, such complete precision, that AnísyaFëdorovna, who had at once handed her the handkerchief she needed for the dance, had tears in her eyes, though she laughed as she watched this slim, graceful countess, reared in silks and velvets and so different from herself, who yet was able to understand all that was in Anísya and in Anísya's father and mother and aunt, and in every Russian man and woman.

"Well, little countess; that's it—come on!" cried "Uncle," with a joyous laugh, having finished the dance. "Well done, niece! Now a fine young fellow must be found as husband for you. That's it—come on!"

"He's chosen already," said Nicholas smiling.

"Oh?" said "Uncle" in surprise, looking inquiringly at Natásha, who nodded her head with a happy smile.

"And such a one!" she said. But as soon as she had said it a new train of thoughts and feelings arose in her. "What did Nicholas' smile mean when he said 'chosen already'? Is he glad of it or not? It is as if he thought my Bolkónski would not approve of or understand our gaiety. But he would understand it all. Where is he now?" she thought, and her face suddenly became serious. But this lasted only a second. "Don't dare to think about it," she said to herself, and sat down again smilingly beside "Uncle," begging him to play something more.

"Uncle" played another song and a valse; then after a pause he cleared his throat and sang his favorite hunting song:

As 'twas growing dark last night Fell the snow so soft and light...

"Uncle" sang as peasants sing, with full and naïve conviction that the whole meaning of a song lies in the words and that the tune comes of itself, and that apart from the words there is no tune, which exists only to give measure to the words. As a result of this the unconsidered tune, like the song of a bird, was extraordinarily good. Natásha was in ecstasies over "Uncle's" singing. She resolved to give up learning the harp and to play only the guitar. She asked "Uncle" for his guitar and at once found the chords of the song.

War and Peace

After nine o'clock two traps and three mounted men, who had been sent to look for them, arrived to fetch Natásha and Pétya. The count and countess did not know where they were and were very anxious, said one of the men.

Pétya was carried out like a log and laid in the larger of the two traps. Natásha and Nicholas got into the other. "Uncle" wrapped Natásha up warmly and took leave of her with quite a new tenderness. He accompanied them on foot as far as the bridge that could not be crossed, so that they had to go round by the ford, and he sent huntsmen to ride in front with lanterns.

"Good-by, dear niece," his voice called out of the darkness—not the voice Natásha had known previously, but the one that had sung *As 'twas growing dark last night.*

In the village through which they passed there were red lights and a cheerful smell of smoke.

"What a darling Uncle is!" said Natásha, when they had come out onto the highroad.

"Yes," returned Nicholas. "You're not cold?"

"No. I'm quite, quite all right. I feel so comfortable!" answered Natásha, almost perplexed by her feelings. They remained silent a long while. The night was dark and damp. They could not see the horses, but only heard them splashing through the unseen mud.

What was passing in that receptive childlike soul that so eagerly caught and assimilated all the diverse impressions of life? How did they all find place in her? But she was very happy. As they were nearing home she suddenly struck up the air of *As 'twas growing dark last night*—the tune of which she had all the way been trying to get and had at last caught.

"Got it?" said Nicholas.

"What were you thinking about just now, Nicholas?" inquired Natásha.

They were fond of asking one another that question.

"I?" said Nicholas, trying to remember. "Well, you see, first I thought that Rugáy, the red hound, was like Uncle, and that if he were a man he would always keep Uncle near him, if not for his riding, then for his manner. What a good fellow Uncle is! Don't you think so?... Well, and you?"

"I? Wait a bit, wait.... Yes, first I thought that we are driving along and imagining that we are going home, but that heaven knows where we are really going in the darkness, and that we shall arrive and suddenly find that we are not in Otrádnoe, but in Fairyland. And then I thought... No, nothing else."

"I know, I expect you thought of him," said Nicholas, smiling as Natásha knew by the sound of his voice.

"No," said Natásha, though she had in reality been thinking about Prince Andrew at the same time as of the rest, and of how he would have liked "Uncle." "And then I was saying to myself all the way, 'How well Anísya carried herself, how well!'" And Nicholas heard her spontaneous, happy, ringing laughter. "And do you know," she suddenly said, "I know that I shall never again be as happy and tranquil as I am now."

"Rubbish, nonsense, humbug!" exclaimed Nicholas, and he thought: "How charming this Natásha of mine is! I have no other friend like her and never shall have. Why should she marry? We might always drive about together!"

"What a darling this Nicholas of mine is!" thought Natásha.

"Ah, there are still lights in the drawing room!" she said, pointing to the windows of the house that gleamed invitingly in the moist velvety darkness of the night.

CHAPTER VIII

Count IlyáRostóv had resigned the position of Marshal of the Nobility because it involved him in too much expense, but still his affairs did not improve. Natásha and Nicholas often noticed their parents conferring together anxiously and privately and heard suggestions of selling the fine ancestral Rostóv house and estate near Moscow. It was not necessary to entertain so freely as when the count had been Marshal, and life at Otrádnoe was quieter than in former years, but still the enormous house and its lodges were full of people and more than twenty sat down to table every day. These were all their own people who had settled down in the house almost as members of the family, or persons who were, it seemed, obliged to live in the count's house. Such were Dimmler the musician and his wife, Vogel the dancing master and his family, Belóva, an old maiden lady, an inmate of the house, and many others such as Pétya's tutors, the girls' former governess, and other people who simply found it preferable and more advantageous to live in the count's house than at home. They had not as many visitors as before, but the old habits of life without which the count and countess could not conceive of existence remained unchanged. There was still the hunting establishment which Nicholas had even enlarged, the same fifty horses and fifteen grooms in the stables, the same expensive presents and dinner parties to the whole district on name days; there were still the count's games of whist and boston, at which—spreading out his cards so that everybody could see them—he let himself be plundered of hundreds of rubles every day by his neighbors, who looked upon an opportunity to play a rubber with Count Rostóv as a most profitable source of income.

The count moved in his affairs as in a huge net, trying not to believe that he was entangled but becoming more and more so at every step, and feeling too feeble to break the meshes or to set to work carefully and patiently to disentangle them. The countess, with her loving heart, felt that her children were being ruined, that it was not the count's fault for he could not help being what he was—that (though he tried to hide it) he himself suffered from the consciousness of his own and his children's ruin, and she tried to find means of remedying the position. From her feminine point of view she could see only one solution, namely, for Nicholas to marry a rich heiress. She felt this to be their last hope and that if Nicholas refused the match she had found for him, she would have to abandon the hope of ever getting matters right. This match was with Julie Karágina, the daughter of excellent and virtuous parents, a girl the Rostóvs had known from childhood, and who had now become a wealthy heiress through the death of the last of her brothers.

The countess had written direct to Julie's mother in Moscow suggesting a marriage between their children and had received a favorable answer from her. Karágina had replied that for her part she was agreeable, and everything depend on her daughter's inclination. She invited Nicholas to come to Moscow.

Several times the countess, with tears in her eyes, told her son that now both her daughters were settled, her only wish was to see him married. She said she could lie down in her grave peacefully if that were accomplished. Then she told him that she knew of a splendid girl and tried to discover what he thought about marriage.

At other times she praised Julie to him and advised him to go to Moscow during the holidays to amuse himself. Nicholas guessed what his mother's remarks were leading to and during one of these conversations induced her to speak quite frankly. She told him that her only hope of getting their affairs disentangled now lay in his marrying Julie Karágina.

"But, Mamma, suppose I loved a girl who has no fortune, would you expect me to sacrifice my feelings and my honor for the sake of money?" he asked his mother, not realizing the cruelty of his question and only wishing to show his noble-mindedness.

"No, you have not understood me," said his mother, not knowing how to justify herself. "You have not understood me, Nikólenka. It is your happiness I wish for," she added, feeling that she was telling an untruth and was becoming entangled. She began to cry.

"Mamma, don't cry! Only tell me that you wish it, and you know I will give my life, anything, to put you at ease," said Nicholas. "I would sacrifice anything for you—even my feelings."

But the countess did not want the question put like that: she did not want a sacrifice from her son, she herself wished to make a sacrifice for him.

"No, you have not understood me, don't let us talk about it," she replied, wiping away her tears.

"Maybe I do love a poor girl," said Nicholas to himself. "Am I to sacrifice my feelings and my honor for money? I wonder how Mamma could speak so to me. Because Sónya is poor I must not love her," he thought, "must not respond to her faithful, devoted love? Yet I should certainly be happier with her than with some doll-like Julie. I can always sacrifice my feelings for my family's welfare," he said to himself, "but I can't coerce my feelings. If I love Sónya, that feeling is for me stronger and higher than all else."

Nicholas did not go to Moscow, and the countess did not renew the conversation with him about marriage. She saw with sorrow, and sometimes with exasperation, symptoms of a growing attachment between her son and the portionless Sónya. Though she blamed herself for it, she could not refrain from grumbling at and worrying Sónya, often pulling her up without reason, addressing her stiffly as "my dear," and using the formal "you" instead of the intimate "thou" in speaking to her. The kindhearted countess was the more vexed with Sónya because that poor, dark-eyed niece of hers was so meek, so kind, so devotedly grateful to her benefactors, and so faithfully, unchangingly, and unselfishly in love with Nicholas, that there were no grounds for finding fault with her.

Nicholas was spending the last of his leave at home. A fourth letter had come from Prince Andrew, from Rome, in which he wrote that he would have been on his way back to Russia long ago had not his wound unexpectedly reopened in the warm climate, which obliged him to defer his return till the beginning of the new year. Natásha was still as much in love with her betrothed, found the same comfort in that love, and was still as ready to throw herself into all the pleasures of life as before; but at the end of the fourth month of their separation she began to have fits of depression which she could not master. She felt sorry for herself: sorry that she was being wasted all this time and of no use to anyone—while she felt herself so capable of loving and being loved.

Things were not cheerful in the Rostóvs' home.

CHAPTER IX

C hristmas came and except for the ceremonial Mass, the solemn and wearisome Christmas congratulations from neighbors and servants, and the new dresses everyone put on, there were no special festivities, though the calm frost of twenty degrees Réaumur, the dazzling sunshine by day, and the starlight of the winter nights seemed to call for some special celebration of the season.

On the third day of Christmas week, after the midday dinner, all the inmates of the house dispersed to various rooms. It was the dullest time of the day. Nicholas, who had been visiting some neighbors that morning, was asleep on the sitting-room sofa. The old count was resting in his study. Sónya sat in the drawing room at the round table, copying a design for embroidery. The countess was playing patience. Nastásyalvánovna the buffoon sat with a sad face at the window with two old ladies. Natásha came into the room, went up to Sónya, glanced at what she was doing, and then went up to her mother and stood without speaking.

"Why are you wandering about like an outcast?" asked her mother. "What do you want?"

"*Him*... I want him... now, this minute! I want *him!*" said Natásha, with glittering eyes and no sign of a smile.

The countess lifted her head and looked attentively at her daughter.

"Don't look at me, Mamma! Don't look; I shall cry directly."

"Sit down with me a little," said the countess.

"Mamma, I want *him*. Why should I be wasted like this, Mamma?"

Her voice broke, tears gushed from her eyes, and she turned quickly to hide them and left the room.

She passed into the sitting room, stood there thinking awhile, and then went into the maids' room. There an old maidservant was grumbling at a young girl who stood panting, having just run in through the cold from the serfs' quarters.

"Stop playing—there's a time for everything," said the old woman.

"Let her alone, Kondrátevna," said Natásha. "Go, Mavrúshka, go."

Having released Mavrúshka, Natásha crossed the dancing hall and went to the vestibule. There an old footman and two young ones were playing cards. They broke off and rose as she entered.

"What can I do with them?" thought Natásha.

"Oh, Nikíta, please go... where can I send him?... Yes, go to the yard and fetch a fowl, please, a cock, and you, Misha, bring me some oats."

"Just a few oats?" said Misha, cheerfully and readily.

"Go, go quickly," the old man urged him.

"And you, Theodore, get me a piece of chalk."

On her way past the butler's pantry she told them to set a samovar, though it was not at all the time for tea.

Fóka, the butler, was the most ill-tempered person in the house. Natásha liked to test her power over him. He distrusted the order and asked whether the samovar was really wanted.

"Oh dear, what a young lady!" said Fóka, pretending to frown at Natásha.

No one in the house sent people about or gave them as much trouble as Natásha did. She could not see people unconcernedly, but had to send them on some errand. She seemed to be trying whether any of them would get angry or sulky with her; but the serfs fulfilled no one's orders so readily as they did hers. "What can I do, where can I go?" thought she, as she went slowly along the passage.

"NastásyaIvánovna, what sort of children shall I have?" she asked the buffoon, who was coming toward her in a woman's jacket.

"Why, fleas, crickets, grasshoppers," answered the buffoon.

"O Lord, O Lord, it's always the same! Oh, where am I to go? What am I to do with myself?" And tapping with her heels, she ran quickly upstairs to see Vogel and his wife who lived on the upper story.

Two governesses were sitting with the Vogels at a table, on which were plates of raisins, walnuts, and almonds. The governesses were discussing whether it was cheaper to live in Moscow or Odessa. Natásha sat down, listened to their talk with a serious and thoughtful air, and then got up again.

"The island of Madagascar," she said, "Ma-da-gas-car," she repeated, articulating each syllable distinctly, and, not replying to Madame Schoss who asked her what she was saying, she went out of the room.

Her brother Pétya was upstairs too; with the man in attendance on him he was preparing fireworks to let off that night.

"Pétya! Pétya!" she called to him. "Carry me downstairs."

Pétya ran up and offered her his back. She jumped on it, putting her arms round his neck, and he pranced along with her.

"No, don't... the island of Madagascar!" she said, and jumping off his back she went downstairs.

Having as it were reviewed her kingdom, tested her power, and made sure that everyone was submissive, but that all the same it was dull, Natásha betook herself to the ballroom, picked up her guitar, sat down in a dark corner behind a bookcase, and began to run her fingers over the strings in the bass, picking out a passage she recalled from an opera she had heard in Petersburg with Prince Andrew. What she drew from the guitar would have had no meaning for other listeners, but in her imagination a whole series of reminiscences arose from those sounds. She sat behind the bookcase with her eyes fixed on a streak of light escaping from the pantry door and listened to herself and pondered. She was in a mood for brooding on the past.

Sónya passed to the pantry with a glass in her hand. Natásha glanced at her and at the crack in the pantry door, and it seemed to her that she remembered the light falling through that crack once before and Sónya passing with a glass in her hand. "Yes it was exactly the same," thought Natásha.

"Sónya, what is this?" she cried, twanging a thick string.

"Oh, you are there!" said Sónya with a start, and came near and listened. "I don't know. A storm?" she ventured timidly, afraid of being wrong.

"There! That's just how she started and just how she came up smiling timidly when all this happened before," thought Natásha, "and in just the same way I thought there was something lacking in her."

"No, it's the chorus from *The Water-Carrier*, listen!" and Natásha sang the air of the chorus so that Sónya should catch it. "Where were you going?" she asked.

"To change the water in this glass. I am just finishing the design."

"You always find something to do, but I can't," said Natásha. "And where's Nicholas?"

"Asleep, I think."

"Sónya, go and wake him," said Natásha. "Tell him I want him to come and sing."

She sat awhile, wondering what the meaning of it all having happened before could be, and without solving this problem, or at all regretting not having done so, she again passed in fancy to the time when she was with *him* and he was looking at her with a lover's eyes.

"Oh, if only he would come quicker! I am so afraid it will never be! And, worst of all, I am growing old—that's the thing! There won't then be in me what there is now. But perhaps he'll come today, will come immediately. Perhaps he has come and is sitting in the drawing room. Perhaps he came yesterday and I have forgotten it." She rose, put down the guitar, and went to the drawing room.

All the domestic circle, tutors, governesses, and guests, were already at the tea table. The servants stood round the table—but Prince Andrew was not there and life was going on as before.

"Ah, here she is!" said the old count, when he saw Natásha enter. "Well, sit down by me." But Natásha stayed by her mother and glanced round as if looking for something.

"Mamma!" she muttered, "give him to me, give him, Mamma, quickly, quickly!" and she again had difficulty in repressing her sobs.

She sat down at the table and listened to the conversation between the elders and Nicholas, who had also come to the table. "My God, my God! The same faces, the same talk, Papa holding his cup and blowing in the same way!" thought Natásha, feeling with horror a sense of repulsion rising up in her for the whole household, because they were always the same.

After tea, Nicholas, Sónya, and Natásha went to the sitting room, to their favorite corner where their most intimate talks always began.

CHAPTER X

"Does it ever happen to you," said Natásha to her brother, when they settled down in the sitting room, "does it ever happen to you to feel as if there were nothing more to come—nothing; that everything good is past? And to feel not exactly dull, but sad?"

"I should think so!" he replied. "I have felt like that when everything was all right and everyone was cheerful. The thought has come into my mind that I was already tired of it all, and that we must all die. Once in the regiment I had not gone to some merrymaking where there was music... and suddenly I felt so depressed..."

"Oh yes, I know, I know, I know!" Natásha interrupted him. "When I was quite little that used to be so with me. Do you remember when I was punished once about some plums? You were all dancing, and I sat sobbing in the schoolroom? I shall never forget it: I felt sad and sorry for everyone, for myself, and for everyone. And I was innocent—that was the chief thing," said Natásha. "Do you remember?"

"I remember," answered Nicholas. "I remember that I came to you afterwards and wanted to comfort you, but do you know, I felt ashamed to. We were terribly absurd. I had a funny doll then and wanted to give it to you. Do you remember?"

"And do you remember," Natásha asked with a pensive smile, "how once, long, long ago, when we were quite little, Uncle called us into the study—that was in the old house—and it was dark—we went in and suddenly there stood..."

"A Negro," chimed in Nicholas with a smile of delight. "Of course I remember. Even now I don't know whether there really was a Negro, or if we only dreamed it or were told about him."

"He was gray, you remember, and had white teeth, and stood and looked at us...."

"Sónya, do *you* remember?" asked Nicholas.

"Yes, yes, I do remember something too," Sónya answered timidly.

"You know I have asked Papa and Mamma about that Negro," said Natásha, "and they say there was no Negro at all. But you see, you remember!"

"Of course I do, I remember his teeth as if I had just seen them."

"How strange it is! It's as if it were a dream! I like that."

"And do you remember how we rolled hard-boiled eggs in the ballroom, and suddenly two old women began spinning round on the carpet? Was that real or not? Do you remember what fun it was?"

"Yes, and you remember how Papa in his blue overcoat fired a gun in the porch?"

So they went through their memories, smiling with pleasure: not the sad memories of old age, but poetic, youthful ones—those impressions of one's most distant past in which dreams and realities blend—and they laughed with quiet enjoyment.

Sónya, as always, did not quite keep pace with them, though they shared the same reminiscences.

Much that they remembered had slipped from her mind, and what she recalled did not arouse the same poetic feeling as they experienced. She simply enjoyed their pleasure and tried to fit in with it.

She only really took part when they recalled Sónya's first arrival. She told them how afraid she had been of Nicholas because he had on a corded jacket and her nurse had told her that she, too, would be sewn up with cords.

"And I remember their telling me that you had been born under a cabbage," said Natásha, "and I remember that I dared not disbelieve it then, but knew that it was not true, and I felt so uncomfortable."

While they were talking a maid thrust her head in at the other door of the sitting room.

"They have brought the cock, Miss," she said in a whisper.

"It isn't wanted, Pólya. Tell them to take it away," replied Natásha.

In the middle of their talk in the sitting room, Dimmler came in and went up to the harp that stood there in a corner. He took off its cloth covering, and the harp gave out a jarring sound.

"Mr. Dimmler, please play my favorite nocturne by Field," came the old countess' voice from the drawing room.

Dimmler struck a chord and, turning to Natásha, Nicholas, and Sónya, remarked: "How quiet you young people are!"

"Yes, we're philosophizing," said Natásha, glancing round for a moment and then continuing the conversation. They were now discussing dreams.

Dimmler began to play; Natásha went on tiptoe noiselessly to the table, took up a candle, carried it out, and returned, seating herself quietly in her former place. It was dark in the room especially where they were sitting on the sofa, but through the big windows the silvery light of the full moon fell on the floor. Dimmler had finished the piece but still sat softly running his fingers over the strings, evidently uncertain whether to stop or to play something else.

"Do you know," said Natásha in a whisper, moving closer to Nicholas and Sónya, "that when one goes on and on recalling memories, one at last begins to remember what happened before one was in the world...."

"That is metempsychosis," said Sónya, who had always learned well, and remembered everything. "The Egyptians believed that our souls have lived in animals, and will go back into animals again."

"No, I don't believe we ever were in animals," said Natásha, still in a whisper though the music had ceased. "But I am certain that we were angels somewhere *there*, and have been here, and that is why we remember...."

"May I join you?" said Dimmler who had come up quietly, and he sat down by them.

"If we have been angels, why have we fallen lower?" said Nicholas. "No, that can't be!"

"Not lower, who said we were lower?... How do I know what I was before?" Natásha rejoined with conviction. "The soul is immortal— well then, if I shall always live I must have lived before, lived for a whole eternity."

"Yes, but it is hard for us to imagine eternity," remarked Dimmler, who had joined the young folk with a mildly condescending smile but now spoke as quietly and seriously as they.

"Why is it hard to imagine eternity?" said Natásha. "It is now today, and it will be tomorrow, and always; and there was yesterday, and the day before...."

"Natásha! Now it's your turn. Sing me something," they heard the countess say. "Why are you sitting there like conspirators?"

"Mamma, I don't at all want to," replied Natásha, but all the same she rose.

None of them, not even the middle-aged Dimmler, wanted to break off their conversation and quit that corner in the sitting room, but Natásha got up and Nicholas sat down at the clavichord. Standing as usual in the middle of the hall and choosing the place where the resonance was best, Natásha began to sing her mother's favorite song.

She had said she did not want to sing, but it was long since she had sung, and long before she again sang, as she did that evening. The count, from his study where he was talking to Mítenka, heard her and, like a schoolboy in a hurry to run out to play, blundered in his talk while giving orders to the steward, and at last stopped, while Mítenka stood in front of him also listening and smiling. Nicholas did not take his eyes off his sister and drew breath in time with her. Sónya, as she listened, thought of the immense difference there was between herself and her friend, and how impossible it was for her to be anything like as bewitching as her cousin. The old countess sat with a blissful yet sad smile and with tears in her eyes, occasionally shaking her head. She thought of Natásha and of her own youth, and of how there was something unnatural and dreadful in this impending marriage of Natásha and Prince Andrew.

Dimmler, who had seated himself beside the countess, listened with closed eyes.

"Ah, Countess," he said at last, "that's a European talent, she has nothing to learn—what softness, tenderness, and strength...."

"Ah, how afraid I am for her, how afraid I am!" said the countess, not realizing to whom she was speaking. Her maternal instinct told her that Natásha had too much of something, and that because of this she would not be happy. Before Natásha had finished singing, fourteen-year-old Pétya rushed in delightedly, to say that some mummers had arrived.

Natásha stopped abruptly.

"Idiot!" she screamed at her brother and, running to a chair, threw herself on it, sobbing so violently that she could not stop for a long time.

"It's nothing, Mamma, really it's nothing; only Pétya startled me," she said, trying to smile, but her tears still flowed and sobs still choked her.

The mummers (some of the house serfs) dressed up as bears, Turks, innkeepers, and ladies—frightening and funny—bringing in with them the cold from outside and a feeling of gaiety, crowded, at first timidly, into the anteroom, then hiding behind one another they pushed into the ballroom where, shyly at first and then more and more merrily and heartily, they started singing, dancing, and playing Christmas games. The countess, when she had identified them and laughed at their costumes, went into the drawing room. The count sat in the ballroom, smiling radiantly and applauding the players. The young people had disappeared.

Half an hour later there appeared among the other mummers in the ballroom an old lady in a hooped skirt—this was Nicholas. A Turkish girl was Pétya. A clown was Dimmler. An hussar was Natásha, and a Circassian was Sónya with burnt-cork mustache and eyebrows.

After the condescending surprise, nonrecognition, and praise, from those who were not themselves dressed up, the young people decided that their costumes were so good that they ought to be shown elsewhere.

Nicholas, who, as the roads were in splendid condition, wanted to take them all for a drive in his troyka, proposed to take with them about a dozen of the serf mummers and drive to "Uncle's."

"No, why disturb the old fellow?" said the countess. "Besides, you wouldn't have room to turn round there. If you must go, go to the Melyukóvs'."

Melyukóva was a widow, who, with her family and their tutors and governesses, lived three miles from the Rostóvs.

"That's right, my dear," chimed in the old count, thoroughly aroused. "I'll dress up at once and go with them. I'll make Pashette open her eyes."

But the countess would not agree to his going; he had had a bad leg all these last days. It was decided that the count must not go, but that if Louisa Ivánovna (Madame Schoss) would go with them, the young ladies might go to the Melyukóvs', Sónya, generally so timid and shy, more urgently than anyone begging Louisa Ivánovna not to refuse.

Sónya's costume was the best of all. Her mustache and eyebrows were extraordinarily becoming. Everyone told her she looked very handsome, and she was in a spirited and energetic mood unusual with her. Some inner voice told her that now or never her fate would be decided, and in her male attire she seemed quite a different person. Louisa Ivánovna consented to go, and in half an hour four troyka sleighs with large and small bells, their runners squeaking and whistling over the frozen snow, drove up to the porch.

Natásha was foremost in setting a merry holiday tone, which, passing from one to another, grew stronger and reached its climax when they all came out into the frost and got into the sleighs, talking, calling to one another, laughing, and shouting.

Two of the troykas were the usual household sleighs, the third was the old count's with a trotter from the Orlóv stud as shaft horse, the fourth was Nicholas' own with a short shaggy black shaft horse. Nicholas, in his old lady's dress over which he had belted his hussar overcoat, stood in the middle of the sleigh, reins in hand.

It was so light that he could see the moonlight reflected from the metal harness disks and from the eyes of the horses, who looked round in alarm at the noisy party under the shadow of the porch roof.

Natásha, Sónya, Madame Schoss, and two maids got into Nicholas' sleigh; Dimmler, his wife, and Pétya, into the old count's, and the rest of the mummers seated themselves in the other two sleighs.

"You go ahead, Zakhár!" shouted Nicholas to his father's coachman, wishing for a chance to race past him.

The old count's troyka, with Dimmler and his party, started forward, squeaking on its runners as though freezing to the snow, its deep-toned bell clanging. The side horses, pressing against the shafts of the middle horse, sank in the snow, which was dry and glittered like sugar, and threw it up.

Nicholas set off, following the first sleigh; behind him the others moved noisily, their runners squeaking. At first they drove at a steady trot along the narrow road. While they drove past the garden the shadows of the bare trees often fell across the road and hid the brilliant moonlight, but as soon as they were past the fence, the snowy plain bathed in moonlight and motionless spread out before them glittering like diamonds and dappled with bluish shadows. *Bang, bang!* went the first sleigh over a cradle hole in the snow of the road, and each of the other sleighs jolted in the same way, and rudely breaking the frost-bound stillness, the troykas began to speed along the road, one after the other.

"A hare's track, a lot of tracks!" rang out Natásha's voice through the frost-bound air.

"How light it is, Nicholas!" came Sónya's voice.

Nicholas glanced round at Sónya, and bent down to see her face closer. Quite a new, sweet face with black eyebrows and mustaches peeped up at him from her sable furs—so close and yet so distant—in the moonlight.

"That used to be Sónya," thought he, and looked at her closer and smiled.

"What is it, Nicholas?"

"Nothing," said he and turned again to the horses.

When they came out onto the beaten highroad—polished by sleigh runners and cut up by rough-shod hoofs, the marks of which were visible in the moonlight—the horses began to tug at the reins of their own accord and increased their pace. The near side horse, arching his head and breaking into a short canter, tugged at his traces. The shaft horse swayed from side to side, moving his ears as if asking: "Isn't it time to begin now?" In front, already far ahead the deep bell of the sleigh ringing farther and farther off, the black horses driven by Zakhár could be clearly seen against the white snow. From that sleigh one could hear the shouts, laughter, and voices of the mummers.

"Gee up, my darlings!" shouted Nicholas, pulling the reins to one side and flourishing the whip.

It was only by the keener wind that met them and the jerks given by the side horses who pulled harder—ever increasing their gallop— that one noticed how fast the troyka was flying. Nicholas looked back. With screams, squeals, and waving of whips that caused even the shaft horses to gallop—the other sleighs followed. The shaft horse swung steadily beneath the bow over its head, with no thought of slackening pace and ready to put on speed when required.

Nicholas overtook the first sleigh. They were driving downhill and coming out upon a broad trodden track across a meadow, near a river.

"Where are we?" thought he. "It's the Kosóy meadow, I suppose. But no—this is something new I've never seen before. This isn't the Kosóy meadow nor the Dëmkin hill, and heaven only knows what it is! It is something new and enchanted. Well, whatever it may be..." And shouting to his horses, he began to pass the first sleigh.

Zakhár held back his horses and turned his face, which was already covered with hoarfrost to his eyebrows.

Nicholas gave the horses the rein, and Zakhár, stretching out his arms, clucked his tongue and let his horses go.

"Now, look out, master!" he cried.

Faster still the two troykas flew side by side, and faster moved the feet of the galloping side horses. Nicholas began to draw ahead. Zakhár, while still keeping his arms extended, raised one hand with the reins.

"No you won't, master!" he shouted.

Nicholas put all his horses to a gallop and passed Zakhár. The horses showered the fine dry snow on the faces of those in the sleigh— beside them sounded quick ringing bells and they caught confused glimpses of swiftly moving legs and the shadows of the troyka they were passing. The whistling sound of the runners on the snow and the voices of girls shrieking were heard from different sides.

Again checking his horses, Nicholas looked around him. They were still surrounded by the magic plain bathed in moonlight and spangled with stars.

"Zakhár is shouting that I should turn to the left, but why to the left?" thought Nicholas. "Are we getting to the Melyukóvs'? Is this Melyukóvka? Heaven only knows where we are going, and heaven knows what is happening to us—but it is very strange and pleasant whatever it is." And he looked round in the sleigh.

"Look, his mustache and eyelashes are all white!" said one of the strange, pretty, unfamiliar people—the one with fine eyebrows and mustache.

"I think this used to be Natásha," thought Nicholas, "and that was Madame Schoss, but perhaps it's not, and this Circassian with the mustache I don't know, but I love her."

"Aren't you cold?" he asked.

They did not answer but began to laugh. Dimmler from the sleigh behind shouted something—probably something funny—but they could not make out what he said.

"Yes, yes!" some voices answered, laughing.

"But here was a fairy forest with black moving shadows, and a glitter of diamonds and a flight of marble steps and the silver roofs of fairy buildings and the shrill yells of some animals. And if this is really Melyukóvka, it is still stranger that we drove heaven knows where and have come to Melyukóvka," thought Nicholas.

It really was Melyukóvka, and maids and footmen with merry faces came running, out to the porch carrying candles.

"Who is it?" asked someone in the porch.

"The mummers from the count's. I know by the horses," replied some voices.

CHAPTER XI

PelagéyaDanílovnaMelyukóva, a broadly built, energetic woman wearing spectacles, sat in the drawing room in a loose dress, surrounded by her daughters whom she was trying to keep from feeling dull. They were quietly dropping melted wax into snow and looking at the shadows the wax figures would throw on the wall, when they heard the steps and voices of new arrivals in the vestibule.

Hussars, ladies, witches, clowns, and bears, after clearing their throats and wiping the hoarfrost from their faces in the vestibule, came into the ballroom where candles were hurriedly lighted. The clown—Dimmler—and the lady—Nicholas—started a dance. Surrounded by the screaming children the mummers, covering their faces and disguising their voices, bowed to their hostess and arranged themselves about the room.

"Dear me! there's no recognizing them! And Natásha! See whom she looks like! She really reminds me of somebody. But Herr Dimmler—isn't he good! I didn't know him! And how he dances. Dear me, there's a Circassian. Really, how becoming it is to dear Sónya. And who is that? Well, you have cheered us up! Nikíta and Vanya—clear away the tables! And we were sitting so quietly. Ha, ha, ha!... The hussar, the hussar! Just like a boy! And the legs!... I can't look at him..." different voices were saying.

Natásha, the young Melyukóvs' favorite, disappeared with them into the back rooms where a cork and various dressing gowns and male garments were called for and received from the footman by bare girlish arms from behind the door. Ten minutes later, all the young Melyukóvs joined the mummers.

PelagéyaDanílovna, having given orders to clear the rooms for the visitors and arranged about refreshments for the gentry and the serfs, went about among the mummers without removing her spectacles, peering into their faces with a suppressed smile and failing to recognize any of them. It was not merely Dimmler and the Rostóvs she failed to recognize, she did not even recognize her own daughters, or her late husband's, dressing gowns and uniforms, which they had put on.

"And who is this?" she asked her governess, peering into the face of her own daughter dressed up as a Kazán-Tartar. "I suppose it is one of the Rostóvs! Well, Mr. Hussar, and what regiment do you serve in?" she asked Natásha. "Here, hand some fruit jelly to the Turk!" she ordered the butler who was handing things round. "That's not forbidden by his law."

Sometimes, as she looked at the strange but amusing capers cut by the dancers, who—having decided once for all that being disguised, no one would recognize them—were not at all shy, PelagéyaDanílovna hid her face in her handkerchief, and her whole stout body shook with irrepressible, kindly, elderly laughter.

"My little Sásha! Look at Sásha!" she said.

After Russian country dances and chorus dances, PelagéyaDanílovna made the serfs and gentry join in one large circle: a ring, a string, and a silver ruble were fetched and they all played games together.

In an hour, all the costumes were crumpled and disordered. The corked eyebrows and mustaches were smeared over the perspiring, flushed, and merry faces. PelagéyaDanílovna began to recognize the mummers, admired their cleverly contrived costumes, and particularly how they suited the young ladies, and she thanked them all for having entertained her so well. The visitors were invited to supper in the drawing room, and the serfs had something served to them in the ballroom.

"Now to tell one's fortune in the empty bathhouse is frightening!" said an old maid who lived with the Melyukóvs, during supper.

"Why?" said the eldest Melyukóv girl.

"You wouldn't go, it takes courage...."

"I'll go," said Sónya.

"Tell what happened to the young lady!" said the second Melyukóv girl.

"Well," began the old maid, "a young lady once went out, took a cock, laid the table for two, all properly, and sat down. After sitting a while, she suddenly hears someone coming... a sleigh drives up with harness bells; she hears him coming! He comes in, just in the shape of a man, like an officer—comes in and sits down to table with her."

"Ah! ah!" screamed Natásha, rolling her eyes with horror.

"Yes? And how... did he speak?"

"Yes, like a man. Everything quite all right, and he began persuading her; and she should have kept him talking till cockcrow, but she got frightened, just got frightened and hid her face in her hands. Then he caught her up. It was lucky the maids ran in just then...."

"Now, why frighten them?" said PelagéyaDanílovna.

"Mamma, you used to try your fate yourself..." said her daughter.

"And how does one do it in a barn?" inquired Sónya.

"Well, say you went to the barn now, and listened. It depends on what you hear; hammering and knocking—that's bad; but a sound of shifting grain is good and one sometimes hears that, too."

"Mamma, tell us what happened to you in the barn."

PelagéyaDanílovna smiled.

"Oh, I've forgotten..." she replied. "But none of you would go?"

"Yes, I will; PelagéyaDanílovna, let me! I'll go," said Sónya.

"Well, why not, if you're not afraid?"

"Louisa Ivánovna, may I?" asked Sónya.

Whether they were playing the ring and string game or the ruble game or talking as now, Nicholas did not leave Sónya's side, and gazed at her with quite new eyes. It seemed to him that it was only today, thanks to that burnt-cork mustache, that he had fully learned to know her. And really, that evening, Sónya was brighter, more animated, and prettier than Nicholas had ever seen her before.

"So that's what she is like; what a fool I have been!" he thought gazing at her sparkling eyes, and under the mustache a happy rapturous smile dimpled her cheeks, a smile he had never seen before.

"I'm not afraid of anything," said Sónya. "May I go at once?" She got up.

They told her where the barn was and how she should stand and listen, and they handed her a fur cloak. She threw this over her head and shoulders and glanced at Nicholas.

"What a darling that girl is!" thought he. "And what have I been thinking of till now?"

Sónya went out into the passage to go to the barn. Nicholas went hastily to the front porch, saying he felt too hot. The crowd of people really had made the house stuffy.

Outside, there was the same cold stillness and the same moon, but even brighter than before. The light was so strong and the snow sparkled with so many stars that one did not wish to look up at the sky and the real stars were unnoticed. The sky was black and dreary, while the earth was gay.

"I am a fool, a fool! what have I been waiting for?" thought Nicholas, and running out from the porch he went round the corner of the house and along the path that led to the back porch. He knew Sónya would pass that way. Halfway lay some snow-covered piles of firewood and across and along them a network of shadows from the bare old lime trees fell on the snow and on the path. This path led to the barn. The log walls of the barn and its snow-covered roof, that looked as if hewn out of some precious stone, sparkled in the moonlight. A tree in the garden snapped with the frost, and then all was again perfectly silent. His bosom seemed to inhale not air but the strength of eternal youth and gladness.

From the back porch came the sound of feet descending the steps, the bottom step upon which snow had fallen gave a ringing creak and he heard the voice of an old maidservant saying, "Straight, straight, along the path, Miss. Only, don't look back."

"I am not afraid," answered Sónya's voice, and along the path toward Nicholas came the crunching, whistling sound of Sónya's feet in her thin shoes.

Sónya came along, wrapped in her cloak. She was only a couple of paces away when she saw him, and to her too he was not the Nicholas she had known and always slightly feared. He was in a woman's dress, with tousled hair and a happy smile new to Sónya. She ran rapidly toward him.

"Quite different and yet the same," thought Nicholas, looking at her face all lit up by the moonlight. He slipped his arms under the cloak that covered her head, embraced her, pressed her to him, and kissed her on the lips that wore a mustache and had a smell of burnt cork. Sónya kissed him full on the lips, and disengaging her little hands pressed them to his cheeks.

"Sónya!... Nicholas!"... was all they said. They ran to the barn and then back again, re-entering, he by the front and she by the back porch.

CHAPTER XII

When they all drove back from PelagéyaDanílovna's, Natásha, who always saw and noticed everything, arranged that she and Madame Schoss should go back in the sleigh with Dimmler, and Sónya with Nicholas and the maids.

On the way back Nicholas drove at a steady pace instead of racing and kept peering by that fantastic all-transforming light into Sónya's face and searching beneath the eyebrows and mustache for his former and his present Sónya from whom he had resolved never to be parted again. He looked and recognizing in her both the old and the new Sónya, and being reminded by the smell of burnt cork of the sensation of her kiss, inhaled the frosty air with a full breast and, looking at the ground flying beneath him and at the sparkling sky, felt himself again in fairyland.

"Sónya, is it well with *thee?*" he asked from time to time.

"Yes!" she replied. "And with *thee?*"

When halfway home Nicholas handed the reins to the coachman and ran for a moment to Natásha's sleigh and stood on its wing.

"Natásha!" he whispered in French, "do you know I have made up my mind about Sónya?"

"Have you told her?" asked Natásha, suddenly beaming all over with joy.

"Oh, how strange you are with that mustache and those eyebrows!... Natásha—are you glad?"

"I am so glad, so glad! I was beginning to be vexed with you. I did not tell you, but you have been treating her badly. What a heart she has, Nicholas! I am horrid sometimes, but I was ashamed to be happy while Sónya was not," continued Natásha. "Now I am so glad! Well, run back to her."

"No, wait a bit.... Oh, how funny you look!" cried Nicholas, peering into her face and finding in his sister too something new, unusual, and bewitchingly tender that he had not seen in her before. "Natásha, it's magical, isn't it?"

"Yes," she replied. "You have done splendidly."

"Had I seen her before as she is now," thought Nicholas, "I should long ago have asked her what to do and have done whatever she told me, and all would have been well."

"So you are glad and I have done right?"

"Oh, quite right! I had a quarrel with Mamma some time ago about it. Mamma said she was angling for you. How could she say such a thing! I nearly stormed at Mamma. I will never let anyone say anything bad of Sónya, for there is nothing but good in her."

"Then it's all right?" said Nicholas, again scrutinizing the expression of his sister's face to see if she was in earnest. Then he jumped down and, his boots scrunching the snow, ran back to his sleigh. The same happy, smiling Circassian, with mustache and beaming eyes looking up from under a sable hood, was still sitting there, and that Circassian was Sónya, and that Sónya was certainly his future happy and loving wife.

When they reached home and had told their mother how they had spent the evening at the Melyukóvs', the girls went to their bedroom. When they had undressed, but without washing off the cork mustaches, they sat a long time talking of their happiness. They talked of how they would live when they were married, how their husbands would be friends, and how happy they would be. On Natásha's table stood two looking glasses which Dunyásha had prepared beforehand.

"Only when will all that be? I am afraid never.... It would be too good!" said Natásha, rising and going to the looking glasses.

"Sit down, Natásha; perhaps you'll see him," said Sónya.

Natásha lit the candles, one on each side of one of the looking glasses, and sat down.

"I see someone with a mustache," said Natásha, seeing her own face.

"You mustn't laugh, Miss," said Dunyásha.

With Sónya's help and the maid's, Natásha got the glass she held into the right position opposite the other; her face assumed a serious expression and she sat silent. She sat a long time looking at the receding line of candles reflected in the glasses and expecting (from tales she had heard) to see a coffin, or *him*, Prince Andrew, in that last dim, indistinctly outlined square. But ready as she was to take the smallest speck for the image of a man or of a coffin, she saw nothing. She began blinking rapidly and moved away from the looking glasses.

"Why is it others see things and I don't?" she said. "You sit down now, Sónya. You absolutely must, tonight! Do it for me.... Today I feel so frightened!"

Sónya sat down before the glasses, got the right position, and began looking.

"Now, Miss Sónya is sure to see something," whispered Dunyásha; "while you do nothing but laugh."

Sónya heard this and Natásha's whisper:

"I know she will. She saw something last year."

For about three minutes all were silent.

"Of course she will!" whispered Natásha, but did not finish... suddenly Sónya pushed away the glass she was holding and covered her eyes with her hand.

"Oh, Natásha!" she cried.

"Did you see? Did you? What was it?" exclaimed Natásha, holding up the looking glass.

Sónya had not seen anything, she was just wanting to blink and to get up when she heard Natásha say, "Of course she will!" She did not wish to disappoint either Dunyásha or Natásha, but it was hard to sit still. She did not herself know how or why the exclamation escaped her when she covered her eyes.

"You saw him?" urged Natásha, seizing her hand.

"Yes. Wait a bit... I... saw him," Sónya could not help saying, not yet knowing whom Natásha meant by *him*, Nicholas or Prince Andrew.

"But why shouldn't I say I saw something? Others do see! Besides who can tell whether I saw anything or not?" flashed through Sónya's mind.

"Yes, I saw him," she said.

"How? Standing or lying?"

"No, I saw... At first there was nothing, then I saw him lying down."

"Andrew lying? Is he ill?" asked Natásha, her frightened eyes fixed on her friend.

"No, on the contrary, on the contrary! His face was cheerful, and he turned to me." And when saying this she herself fancied she had really seen what she described.

"Well, and then, Sónya?..."

"After that, I could not make out what there was; something blue and red...."

"Sónya! When will he come back? When shall I see him! O, God, how afraid I am for him and for myself and about everything!..." Natásha began, and without replying to Sónya's words of comfort she got into bed, and long after her candle was out lay open-eyed and motionless, gazing at the moonlight through the frosty windowpanes.

CHAPTER XIII

S oon after the Christmas holidays Nicholas told his mother of his love for Sónya and of his firm resolve to marry her. The countess, who had long noticed what was going on between them and was expecting this declaration, listened to him in silence and then told her son that he might marry whom he pleased, but that neither she nor his father would give their blessing to such a marriage. Nicholas, for the first time, felt that his mother was displeased with him and that, despite her love for him, she would not give way. Coldly, without looking at her son, she sent for her husband and, when he came, tried briefly and coldly to inform him of the facts, in her son's presence, but unable to restrain herself she burst into tears of vexation and left the room. The old count began irresolutely to admonish Nicholas and beg him to abandon his purpose. Nicholas replied that he could not go back on his word, and his father, sighing and evidently disconcerted, very soon became silent and went in to the countess. In all his encounters with his son, the count was always conscious of his own guilt toward him for having wasted the family fortune, and so he could not be angry with him for refusing to marry an heiress and choosing the dowerless Sónya. On this occasion, he was only more vividly conscious of the fact that if his affairs had not been in disorder, no better wife for Nicholas than Sónya could have been wished for, and that no one but himself with his Mítenka and his uncomfortable habits was to blame for the condition of the family finances.

The father and mother did not speak of the matter to their son again, but a few days later the countess sent for Sónya and, with a cruelty neither of them expected, reproached her niece for trying to catch Nicholas and for ingratitude. Sónya listened silently with downcast eyes to the countess' cruel words, without understanding what was required of her. She was ready to sacrifice everything for her benefactors. Self-sacrifice was her most cherished idea but in this case she could not see what she ought to sacrifice, or for whom. She could not help loving the countess and the whole Rostóv family, but neither could she help loving Nicholas and knowing that his happiness depended on that love. She was silent and sad and did not reply. Nicholas felt the situation to be intolerable and went to have an explanation with his mother. He first implored her to forgive him and Sónya and consent to their marriage, then he threatened that if she molested Sónya he would at once marry her secretly.

The countess, with a coldness her son had never seen in her before, replied that he was of age, that Prince Andrew was marrying without his father's consent, and he could do the same, but that she would never receive that *intriguer* as her daughter.

Exploding at the word *intriguer*, Nicholas, raising his voice, told his mother he had never expected her to try to force him to sell his feelings, but if that were so, he would say for the last time.... But he had no time to utter the decisive word which the expression of his face caused his mother to await with terror, and which would perhaps have forever remained a cruel memory to them both. He had not time to say it, for Natásha, with a pale and set face, entered the room from the door at which she had been listening.

"Nicholas, you are talking nonsense! Be quiet, be quiet, be quiet, I tell you!..." she almost screamed, so as to drown his voice.

"Mamma darling, it's not at all so... my poor, sweet darling," she said to her mother, who conscious that they had been on the brink of a rupture gazed at her son with terror, but in the obstinacy and excitement of the conflict could not and would not give way.

"Nicholas, I'll explain to you. Go away! Listen, Mamma darling," said Natásha.

Her words were incoherent, but they attained the purpose at which she was aiming.

The countess, sobbing heavily, hid her face on her daughter's breast, while Nicholas rose, clutching his head, and left the room.

Natásha set to work to effect a reconciliation, and so far succeeded that Nicholas received a promise from his mother that Sónya should not be troubled, while he on his side promised not to undertake anything without his parents' knowledge.

Firmly resolved, after putting his affairs in order in the regiment, to retire from the army and return and marry Sónya, Nicholas, serious, sorrowful, and at variance with his parents, but, as it seemed to him, passionately in love, left at the beginning of January to rejoin his regiment.

After Nicholas had gone things in the Rostóv household were more depressing than ever, and the countess fell ill from mental agitation.

Sónya was unhappy at the separation from Nicholas and still more so on account of the hostile tone the countess could not help adopting toward her. The count was more perturbed than ever by the condition of his affairs, which called for some decisive action. Their town house and estate near Moscow had inevitably to be sold, and for this they had to go to Moscow. But the countess' health obliged them to delay their departure from day to day.

Natásha, who had borne the first period of separation from her betrothed lightly and even cheerfully, now grew more agitated and impatient every day. The thought that her best days, which she would have employed in loving him, were being vainly wasted, with no advantage to anyone, tormented her incessantly. His letters for the most part irritated her. It hurt her to think that while she lived only in the thought of him, he was living a real life, seeing new places and new people that interested him. The more interesting his letters were the more vexed she felt. Her letters to him, far from giving her any comfort, seemed to her a wearisome and artificial obligation. She could not write, because she could not conceive the possibility of expressing sincerely in a letter even a thousandth part of what she expressed by voice, smile, and glance. She wrote to him formal, monotonous, and dry letters, to which she attached no importance herself, and in the rough copies of which the countess corrected her mistakes in spelling.

There was still no improvement in the countess' health, but it was impossible to defer the journey to Moscow any longer. Natásha'strousseau had to be ordered and the house sold. Moreover, Prince Andrew was expected in Moscow, where old Prince Bolkónski was spending the winter, and Natásha felt sure he had already arrived.

So the countess remained in the country, and the count, taking Sónya and Natásha with him, went to Moscow at the end of January.